英語聽&說

高級篇

白野伊津夫
Lisa A. Stefani 著

何信彰・鄭惠雯 譯

CD
BOOK

LISTENING & SPEAKING
STRATEGIES
ADVANCED COURSE

三民書局

前　言

　　本書《英語聽＆說》系列共四冊，分別為「入門篇」「初級篇」「中級篇」和「高級篇」。本「高級篇」是此系列的最後一冊，目的希望學習者在以之前的三冊為基礎培養實力後，能多加提高運用英語的能力，即再訓練難度更高的英語聽與說的表達能力。本冊的程度是大學以上，同時考量到商業英語的重要性，故於英語的日常會話之外，也大量增加商業英語會話，很適合具有相當英文程度的人及貿易人士用來提高英語能力。

　　本系列編輯的基本理念在於強調「會話從聽開始」的逆向思考方式。於前三冊「入門篇」「初級篇」和「中級篇」的前言中，曾分別舉愛迪生發明電燈泡、氫氧能源發電原理及野口悠紀雄先生的超整理法，來說明逆向思考的重要性。人類藉由逆向思考，帶來劃時代的發明，同時改變了世界。再舉一例日常生活所見的事物說明：我們身上穿的衣服大多是由縫紉機所縫製，這個縫紉機也是依逆向思考所產生。未有縫紉機之前，我們是用手穿針線，將線戳進針的尾端略粗的部位；而縫紉機卻是相反，是將線穿過針的尖頭部位，這種逆向思考的發明使得人類可以方便利用機器縫製衣服。

　　逆向思考也能在英語的學習上帶來良好的效果。傳統的學習方式是「從說開始」，注重完整背誦某一情境下可能派得上用場的會話句子。但有經驗的人都知道，一旦要用英語應對實際狀況時，卻往往說不出記在腦海裡的句子。不論多麼用功地反覆背誦，英語會話就是無法有明顯的進步，原因在於這種方法正違背人類學習語言的自然過程。若想將英語說得很溜，就應該像小孩學習母親講話一樣──「從聽開始」。異國婚姻下或海外歸國的小孩，

其外語能力之所以強，就是長期在聽的環境下學習語言的緣故；他們或是跟隨父母親，或是從與當地的小孩一起遊玩讀書的過程中培養聽力。聽力與口語表達能力有著密不可分的關係，聽力若提升，口語表達能力必定也能大幅度地進步。

但是到了大人階段，往往容易因無法理解對方所說的話而感到不安與害怕，這一點正是造成英語會話能力進步的障礙。不管對方說什麼，皆回答 Yes 或傻笑地當場敷衍過去，這將會產生挫折感，不僅無心期待下一次的對話，還會刻意避開任何與外國人輕鬆閒聊的機會。相反地，當培養並提升聽力後，在與外國人士對話時，就能接收（input）對方所說的話語，記在腦海裡；以後遇到適當的時機，就能化作自己的話語傳送（output）出去。而且，有良好的聽力可以聽懂電視及廣播電台的即時資訊，也能簡單順利地將聽到的內容融入於日常會話之中。尤其在與多數外國人同時對談的場合中，更需具備良好的聽力，若無法理解正常速度下的英文，就無法順利進行溝通。

衷心希望「英語會話從聽開始」這一座右銘可以激勵各位精進學習，無論在日常生活中或商場上都能廣泛靈活運用英語。

最後，謹向經常給予建議及鼓勵的研究社出版部佐藤淳先生，以及協助完成本書的鈴井加奈子小姐，致上感謝之意。

白野伊津夫

Lisa A. Stefani

目　次

前言
本書使用方法

本書使用方法

本書共十五章，各章分 **Listening** 及 **Speaking** 兩大部分。Listening 的部分有四個小單元，Speaking 的部分則由五個小單元組成。

Listening

首先出現的「**Warm-up/Pre-questions**」是測驗在聽完各章主題下的英文短文後，能聽懂多少內容的選擇題。請聽完 CD 播放一次後立即作答。正確作答的要訣在於注意聆聽內容中涵蓋的重要訊息。由於是聽力的熱身運動，所以可以輕鬆面對。

會話的聽力練習則分成三個步驟，讓學習者循序漸進檢驗自己對內容的理解度。「**Listening Step 1**」是透過選擇題，練習粗略抓住初次聽到的會話內容概要。請聽完 CD 播放一次後立即作答。只要理解會話的大概內容，順著會話的進展，就能獲得正確的解答，不需在意細節，掌握住內容的要點即可。

「**Listening Step 2**」是練習正確聽懂會話中涵蓋的重要訊息。首先要自我檢測是否能完全了解會話中出現的關鍵字意義，再開始做聽力的填空練習，以練習正確聽出句中的特定單字。之後，再聽一次會話並回答兩個問題。聽力秘訣在於掌握 5W1H 中的 who, what, when, where 的要點。

「**Listening Step 3**」是培養完全聽懂會話內容的能力，以及練習判斷會話主角行為的原因和預測將來會如何發展。首先，先自我檢測是否理解會話中出現的片語和重要語句的意義，緊接著做聽力的填空練習，幫助聽懂之前出現過的片語和重要語句。最後，再聽一次會話並回答三個問題。正確解題技巧在於將焦點擺在 5W1H 中的 why 和 how 作答。

　　此部分的「**會話**」(dialog) 可說是該章的重點，介紹該章的主題內容。首先，請先默念會話內容理解意思，若有不懂的地方再看「中譯」或「語法」說明。接下來聽 CD，充分掌握英語的發音、節奏及語調後再發出聲音朗讀。朗讀時，最好是將自己融入為會話主角，並確認自己的英語是否與 CD 播放的英語一樣流暢。建議可以採取聽 CD 後朗誦、朗誦後聽 CD 的間歇式 (interval) 練習法學習。若對發音有自信，也可以採用投影練習法 (shadow training)，這是緊跟著 CD 馬上覆誦的有效學習法。練習完之後，可以切掉開關，試著一個人大聲唸，看看自己的發音是否接近 CD 中外國人的腔調。相信經過這一連串的練習，至少可誦唸 20 到 30 次的會話，結果必能幫助脫口說出自然流利的英語。

　　「**Speaking Function**」中會提供不同的說法來表達相同的意思。例如要向對方確認自己是否了解對方所說的話時，會以英文 I'm not sure I understand. Does that mean...? 詢問，這句話其實可以另外替換成 Do you mean...? / So what you mean is... Right? / In other words, ... Right? 或 So am I right in saying...? 等等。關於相似句的用法及其在語感上有什麼不同，可以參照「解說」中的說明。請務必仔細聽 CD，做好後續練習的準備。

　　「**代換、角色扮演**」是練習流利說出在「Speaking Function」中學得的各種替換句。首先，「代換」練習是邊看 Function 的基本句，邊聽 CD 再大聲唸出代換詞句的部分，請反覆練習直到可以順口說出 Function 的英語句子來。「角色扮演」是視 CD 為談話對象的練習，先注意聆聽完整的對話示範，然後當聽到嗶一聲後即說出適切的英語對應。剛開始可以看書說，但希望經過幾次練習後能不用看書而立即回答。

「**覆誦重要語句**」的單元是希望學習者再度熟習會話中出現的重要用語。在清楚了解重要用語的意義之後，聆聽 CD 並緊跟其後大聲唸出英文句子來。請反覆練習直到可以流利說出。

　　最後的「**實力測驗**」則是提供某一情境，讓學習者自我檢驗是否能就該章所學說出流利的應用語句對應。若是能立即回答三種不同的說法，即是及格，可以證明自己有不錯的學習能力。

A Typical Weekend 典型的週末

Listening

Warm-up / Pre-questions

 請聽《Track 1》的廣告後回答下面問題。

飯店住宿費用裡頭還包含下列哪一項?
  (A) 參加晚宴的費用
  (B) 網路撥接費
  (C) 早餐費

內容 Isn't it about time you took a relaxing weekend getaway? Great Western's weekend rates can't be beat. In addition, a mouthwatering breakfast is included in the rate—fresh fruit, fluffy eggs, specialty omelets, light waffles, crispy bacon and much more.

At Great Western, you will find a great bed, a great rate, and a great breakfast. There has never been a greater reason to take a relaxing weekend getaway. See your travel agent or contact us at 1–800–492–7801. We are also just a click away at www.CreatWestern.com.

中譯 想要過個輕鬆愉快的週末嗎? 威斯坦大飯店推出絕無僅有的週末超低優惠! 另外還附上讓您口水直流的豐盛早餐 —— 新鮮水果、鬆軟的雞蛋、特製煎蛋捲、軟綿綿的格子鬆餅、酥脆的培根, 應有盡有。

威斯坦大飯店提供您舒適的寢具、超低的消費, 以及美味的早

餐。想要享受輕鬆愉快的週末嗎？那還等什麼？請速洽各大旅行社，或撥 1–800–492–7801 與我們聯絡，也可以上網到 www.GreatWestern.com 查詢相關訊息。

解答　(C)

解說　「It is time + 主詞 + 過去式」是假設語氣的句型之一，意指「是該做…的時候了」，而 Isn't it about time you took a relaxing weekend getaway? 是其問句用法。其他字義如下：getaway「短期休假」、rate「費用」、beat「擊敗，勝過」、mouthwatering「讓人口水直流的」、fluffy「鬆軟的」、specialty「特製品」、light「軟綿綿的」、crispy「酥脆的」、travel agent「旅行社」, click 為「按，點選」之意。

Listening Step 1

 請聽《Track 2》的會話後回答下面問題。

> 兩人正在談論什麼話題？
>   (A) 週末假期計畫
>   (B) 美術展覽
>   (C) 攀岩
>
> ---
> 解答 　　　　　　　　　　　　　　　　　　　　　　　　　　(A)

Listening Step 2

熟悉下列關鍵字

> hardly　幾乎不
> rock-climbing　攀岩
> suggest　提議

coast　海岸
winery　葡萄酒釀造廠
art gallery　畫廊；美術館
budget　預算

① 請聽《Track 3》並在括弧內填入正確答案。

1. I can (　　　) wait until Friday so we can have the weekend off.
2. Shall we go rock-(　　　) again?
3. Okay then, what do you (　　　)?
4. Why don't we drive up the (　　　) and visit Philip and Anne?
5. We can even go in the art (　　　) there if you would like.

解答

1. I can (hardly) wait until Friday so we can have the weekend off.
2. Shall we go rock-(climbing) again?
3. Okay then, what do you (suggest)?
4. Why don't we drive up the (coast) and visit Philip and Anne?
5. We can even go in the art (gallery) there if you would like.

① 請再聽一次《Track 2》的會話後回答下面問題。

1. 這位女士提出什麼建議？
   (A) 沿著海岸開車兜風並探望親戚
   (B) 沿著海岸開車兜風並造訪艾瑪鎮
   (C) 造訪幾家釀酒廠
2. 兩人要到哪裡住宿？

(A) 親戚家

(B) 飯店

(C) 露營地

解答   1. (A)   2. (B)

Listening Step 3

熟悉下列語句

drag by （時間）過得很慢

anything but   除了~之外都可以；絕不

be up for   有意；對~有興趣

in a row   連續

drive up the coast   沿著海岸開車

in months   數個月之久

You might be on to something here.   你想到的點子不錯。

not too long of a drive   開車不會太久

That would be fun.   那一定很有趣。

and besides   而且，此外

it's been a while since...   自從…之後已有一段時間了

It's settled.   就這麼決定了。

①請聽《Track 4》並在括弧內填入正確答案。

1. This week is certainly (   ) (   ).

2. No, I'm not really (   ) (   ) that two weekends in a row.

3. I haven't seen my cousin (   ) (   ).

4. Three hours is not too long (   ) (   ) (   ).

5. That (　　) (　　) (　　).

1. This week is certainly (dragging) (by).

2. No, I'm not really (up) (for) that two weekends in a row.

3. I haven't seen my cousin (in) (months).

4. Three hours is not too long (of) (a) (drive).

5. That (would) (be) (fun).

① 請再聽一次《Track 2》的會話後回答下面問題。

1. 這位女士為什麼不想去攀岩？
   (A) 因為怕勞累
   (B) 因為上個禮拜去過了
   (C) 因為身體不太舒服

2. 提到艾瑪鎮時，下列哪一個地方並未出現在會話中？
   (A) 釀酒廠
   (B) 畫廊
   (C) 水族館

3. 兩人為什麼決定住在威斯坦大飯店？
   (A) 週末住宿費用便宜，而且男士一直很喜歡這家飯店的早餐
   (B) 設備完善，而且服務人員的態度很親切
   (C) 不僅住宿費用便宜，在交通上也很方便

解答　　　　　　　　　　　　1. (B)　2. (C)　3. (A)

Speaking

會話

 請再聽一次《Track 2》。

Jason: This week is certainly dragging by. I can't believe it's only Wednesday.

Shelly: I know. I can hardly wait until Friday so we can have the weekend off.

Jason: Me too. What do you want to do this weekend, Shelly?

Shelly: Anything but work!

Jason: I know what you mean. All of these overtime hours are killing me.

Shelly: That's true, but at least we have some extra cash to have fun with. What should we do?

Jason: Shall we go rock-climbing again?

Shelly: No, I'm not really up for that two weekends in a row.

Jason: Okay then, what do you suggest?

Shelly: Why don't we drive up the coast and visit Philip and Anne?

Jason: I haven't seen my cousin in months. You might be on to something here.

Shelly: I think so. The drive up the coast would be fun—and three hours is not too long of a drive.

Jason: No, it's not. We could stop in that little town, El Marr, on the way up and go to the cheesecake shop and the winery. We can even go in the art gallery there if you would like.

Shelly: That would be fun. We can stay at the Great Western because I know you love their breakfasts so much and besides, they have great weekend rates.

Jason: That's true. We can have a relaxing time and stay within our entertainment budget.

Shelly: Let's do it. It's been a while since we've had a weekend getaway.

Jason: Okay. It's settled. I will make the reservations tomorrow. Now I really can't wait until Friday!

Shelly: Me neither!

中 譯 ....

傑生：這禮拜過得好慢，真不敢相信今天才禮拜三而已。

雪莉：沒錯，真希望禮拜五快點來，這樣就可以放假了。

傑生：我也希望。雪莉，這個週末妳要做什麼？

雪莉：別叫我工作就好！

傑生：我也有同感。最近加班真是折磨人。

雪莉：的確，但至少我們有額外的現金可以好好享受一下。玩什麼好呢？

傑生：還要再去攀岩嗎？

雪莉：不要，我不想連續兩個禮拜都去攀岩。

傑生：好吧，那妳有什麼建議？

雪莉：我們可以沿著海岸開車兜風，順便去找菲力浦和安妮。

傑生：我已經好幾個月沒看到我堂弟了。妳想到的主意很不錯。

雪莉：對呀。沿著海岸兜風一定很有趣，而且開三個小時的車也

不算太久。

傑生：沒錯。中途還可以在艾瑪小鎮停留一下，到起司蛋糕店、
釀酒廠逛一逛，甚至也可以參觀畫廊，如果妳想去的話。

雪莉：一定會很好玩。我們可以住在威斯坦大飯店，我知道你最
喜歡這家飯店的早餐了，而且他們週末還有特價優惠。

傑生：對啊，我們可以好好放鬆一下，又不會超出我們的玩樂預
算。

雪莉：就這麼辦，我們已經有一陣子沒好好過週末了。

傑生：好，就這麼說定了。我明天就訂房。真等不及禮拜五了！

雪莉：我也是！

語 法

- drive up the coast （沿著海岸開車）

  介系詞 up 除了表「向～上」之外，也有「沿著（道路等）」的意思。
  另外，對說話者來說，也含有「向遠方去」的語感存在。

  Drive *up* Sunset St. for about ten blocks.

  （沿著日落大道開十個街區左右。）

- in months （數個月之久）

  若介系詞 in 和 not, first, only 及表最高級的字一起造句時，則有「在
  ～期間」的意思。

  I haven't seen my cousin *in* months.

  （我已經好幾個月沒見到我堂弟了。）

  It is the biggest typhoon *in* ten years. （這是十年來最強烈的颱風。）

- weekend rates （週末價格）

  rate 是指按一定比率計算出來的「費用」，如 hotel rates（旅館房間費
  用）、postal rates（郵資）、railroad rates（鐵路運費）等。另外，price
  是指東西買賣的「價格」；cost 是針對為完成某事物所須花費的時間
  與勞力而支付的「代價」；charge 是服務行為等的「價錢」；fare 則是

指交通工具的「票價」。

● It's been a while since we've had a weekend getaway.
（離我們上一次的週末假期已經有好一陣子了。）
美式英語會在 since 的子句中使用現在完成式。

It's been two years since I've taken a vacation.（我已經兩年沒度假了。）

Speaking Function 1

表示提議的說法

請聽《Track 5》。

1. A: Shall we go surfing over the weekend?

   B: Why not? I haven't done it in weeks.

2. A: What about taking our kids to the new amusement park on Saturday?

   B: I think it's a great idea. They will love the rides and games there.

3. A: We could go to a nice resort and enjoy golfing or something.

   B: That would be fun.

解說

● 提議的基本句型為 Shall we ～? 和 Let's ～., 其他還有 Why don't you ～? 及 Why don't we ～?, 留意這兩個句型表面上雖是疑問句, 但並非用來詢問理由。另外, 與熟人之間可以使用 Why not ～? 提議, 例如在百貨公司想建議好友試穿衣服時, 可以說 Why not try it on?。若要說得更鄭重禮貌, 可以使用 Would you care to ～? 或 Would it be an idea to ～?。

● What about ～? 和 How about ～? 也是提議的句型。How about ～?

是比較口語、隨意的用法。留意 about 之後須接名詞或動名詞，
例如：What about going to the beach? 和 How about a walk?。

● 想委婉地提出建議時，可以用 could 或 might as well 表達。could
有「可能的話可以」，might as well 有「也可以，不妨」之意。相
反地，若想直接提出建議，可以說 I suggest～或 I would like to
suggest～。

練習 1【代換】

 請隨《Track 6》做代換練習。

1. *Shall we*   stop on the way and visit one of the wineries?

     Why don't we
     Why not
     Would you care to

2. What about *visiting your mother in Oakland over the weekend?*

     stopping at one of these wineries?
     taking a sunset cruise?
     having dinner at the new Thai restaurant downtown?

3. *We could*   spend our vacation on a ranch and take horseback riding lessons.

     Let's
     We might as well
     I suggest that we

練習 2【角色扮演】

①請隨《Track 7》在嗶一聲後唸出灰色部分的句子。

1. A: Shall we go to New England for the holidays?

   B: Great idea. I've never been there before.

2. A: What about taking our kids to Sea World on Sunday?

   B: That's good. They will enjoy seeing the killer whales, sea lions and penguins.

3. A: We could go to the mountain and enjoy skiing.

   B: That would be fun.

練習 3【覆誦重要語句】

①請隨《Track 8》覆誦英文句子。

1. drag by   「(時間) 過得很慢」

   ↳Today is really dragging by. It's still two o'clock.

   (今天的時間過得好慢，現在才兩點。)

2. can hardly wait   「等不及」

   ↳I can hardly wait to see the game between the Lakers and the Bulls this Friday.

   (我已經等不及要看禮拜五湖人隊和公牛隊的比賽了。)

3. anything but   「除了～之外都可以；絕不」

   ↳I'm for anything but karaoke.

   (只要不是卡拉 OK 我都贊成。)

4. be up for   「有意；對～有興趣」

   ↳He is not really up for a golf tournament with his co-workers. (他不是很想跟同事比高爾夫球。)

5. in a row 「連續」
   ↳ The tennis player once won 75 matches in a row.
   （這名網球選手曾經連續贏 75 場比賽。）

6. in months 「數個月之久」
   ↳ I haven't gone to the movies in years.
   （我已經好幾年沒去看電影了。）

7. not too long of 「～不會太久」
   ↳ Seven hours is not too long of a flight.
   （七個小時的飛行不算太久。）

8. on the way 「途中」
   ↳ Shall we visit a winery on the way and pick up a few
   bottles of wine?（我們途中可以去釀酒廠買幾瓶酒嗎?）

9. rate 「費用」
   ↳ The hotel rates are rather low and they also offer weekly
   discount rates.
   （這家旅館的費用相當低，而且每週還提供折扣。）

10. It's settled. 「就這麼決定了。」
   ↳ It's settled then. We'll go to Magic Mountain for the
   weekend.（那就這麼決定，我們這個週末去魔術山樂園。）

實力測驗

你正和同事們商量國外旅行的事，由於大家都去過美國及歐洲，所以
這次你想提議到陌生的國度土耳其遊玩。請試著用三種不同的說法建
議。

| Chapter 2 | **Problems and Solutions** | 問題與
解決辦法 |

Listening

Warm-up / Pre-questions

 請聽《Track 9》的新聞報導後回答下面問題。

下列哪一項是問題的重點?
(A) 勞工技術水準降低
(B) 基層勞工缺乏
(C) 大學畢業生失業率增加

內容 Entry-level workers are hard to come by these days. Many companies are complaining that there just aren't enough bodies around to fill the positions available. Industries such as restaurant, retail sales, and manufacturing have been hit the hardest since the majority of their needed work force is entry level.

So where have all of the entry-level workers gone? In many cases they've gone on to college or technical school. Few high school graduates are happy earning the minimum wage paid by entry-level positions. Instead, graduations are up and college enrollment has increased by 22% over the last two years.

中譯 最近基層的勞工還真是不好找,許多公司行號抱怨人手不夠,很多職位出缺。其中餐飲、零售、製造等業者最需要的就是這種勞動力,因此所受的衝擊最為嚴重。

究竟這些基層的勞動力都到哪裡去了? 其中很多都跑去念大學

或者技術學校。沒幾個高中畢業生願意從事最基層的工作，領取微薄的基本工資。反倒是過去兩年來，高中畢業的人數增加，而註冊念大專院校的人數也成長了 22%。

解答　(B)

解說　entry-level worker 是指「基層勞工，無經驗的勞工」。其他字義：hard to come by「難以得到的」、complain「抱怨」、industry「產業」、retail sales「零售業」、manufacturing「製造業」、go on to college「進大學」、technical school「技術學校」、minimum wage「最低工資」、graduation「畢業」，enrollment 則為「註冊人數」之意。

Listening Step 1

① 請聽《Track 10》的會話後回答下面問題。

這家餐廳出現了什麼問題？
　(A) 顧客減少
　(B) 衛生不佳
　(C) 人手不夠

解答　　　　　　　　　　　　　　　　　　　　　　　　　　　(C)

Listening Step 2

熟悉下列關鍵字

---

function　運行；起作用
properly　恰當地；正確地
response　回應
fill out　填寫（表格）

```
application    申請表
frustrated    氣餒的，沮喪的
applicant    應徵者
hire    雇用
expertise    專門的技術，專門的知識
existing employee    目前的員工
threaten    威脅
quit    辭職
attitude    態度
process    過程
relief    （痛苦、負擔等的）減輕
post    公告，張貼
```

1 請聽《Track 11》並在括弧內填入正確答案。

1. I just don't know how we can continue to (　　　) like this.

2. I am disappointed in the (　　　).

3. How many people have filled out (　　　)?

4. They haven't (　　　) to quit, have they?

5. I will let them know today when I (　　　) the new schedule.

解答

1. I just don't know how we can continue to (function) like this.

2. I am disappointed in the (responses).

3. How many people have filled out (applications)?

4. They haven't (threatened) to quit, have they?

5. I will let them know today when I (post) the new schedule.

① 請再聽一次《Track 10》的會話後回答下面問題。

1. 這家餐廳的徵人廣告已經張貼多久了?
   (A) 一個禮拜
   (B) 兩個禮拜
   (C) 三個禮拜
2 目前已經有幾個人來應徵?
   (A) 兩個人
   (B) 十個人
   (C) 二十個人

解答　　　　　　　　　　　　　　　1. (C)　2. (A)

Listening Step 3

熟悉下列語句

run a restaurant　經營餐廳
run an advertisement　刊登廣告
so far　到目前為止
That is why...　那就是…的原因; 所以才…
regardless of　不管; 不顧
at this point　現在, 此刻
be aware of　察覺到; 知道

① 請聽《Track 12》並在括弧內填入正確答案。

1. Just two (　　　) (　　　).
2. That (　　　) (　　　) I am so frustrated.
3. I think you should hire them both (　　　) (　　　)

training or expertise.

4. We just need bodies (　　　) (　　　) (　　　).

5. They're very (　　　) (　　　) the problems we're having.

1 請再聽一次《Track 10》的會話後回答下面問題。

1. 會話中的兩個人對於徵人的結果有什麼看法？
   (A) 感到非常滿意
   (B) 認為結果是理所當然的
   (C) 感到失望

2. 經營者打算如何招募新人？
   (A) 提高採用新人的標準
   (B) 只雇用可以配合加班的人
   (C) 不管有無受過訓練或具備專業技術，一律採用

3. 目前餐廳的員工對於工作有什麼看法？
   (A) 抱怨加班太多
   (B) 抱怨薪水太低
   (C) 擔心有一天會被解雇

Speaking

會話

 請再聽一次《Track 10》。

David: I just don't know how we can continue to function like this.

Manager: What seems to be the problem?

David: The same problem we've had for the last three weeks—we don't have enough people to run this restaurant properly.

Manager: I know, David. I have run advertisements for the last three weeks trying to find some new help and I am disappointed in the responses.

David: How many people have filled out applications?

Manager: Just two so far.

David: You must be kidding! We've had only two people who responded to three weeks of advertisements?

Manager: That's right. That is why I am so frustrated.

David: Did you interview the applicants?

Manager: They both have interviews tomorrow.

David: Well, I think you should hire them both regardless of training or expertise. We just need bodies at this point.

Manager: I know. We can't keep our existing employees working so much overtime.

David: Many of them have already started to complain.

Manager: They haven't threatened to quit, have they?

David: No, I haven't heard that yet, but they're very aware of the problems we're having and that doesn't help their attitude about working here.

Manager: Just let them know that we're in the interview process now and they should get some relief soon.

David: I will let them know today when I post the new schedule.

中 譯 ....

大衛: 真不知道這樣要怎麼經營下去。

經理: 出了什麼問題?

大衛: 老問題了,過去三個禮拜我們的人手都不夠,餐廳沒辦法正常營運。

經理: 大衛,這我知道。過去三個禮拜我都有刊登廣告,希望能找到一些幫手,不過反應卻讓人大失所望。

大衛: 有多少人填過應徵表格?

經理: 到目前為止只有兩個。

大衛: 開什麼玩笑!廣告三個禮拜卻只有兩個人應徵?

經理: 沒錯,所以我很氣餒。

大衛: 那來應徵的人你面試過了嗎?

經理: 他們都是明天來面試。

大衛: 嗯,我覺得你應該兩個都錄取,不必管是否受過訓練或具備專業技術,在這個節骨眼只要有人就好了。

經理: 對啊,也不能老是叫目前的員工加班。

大衛: 很多員工已經開始抱怨了。

經理: 但還不至於揚言要辭職吧?

大衛: 這倒還沒聽說,不過他們對公司的問題清楚得很,並沒有

改善他們對於在此工作的態度。

經理：只要讓他們知道我們已經在進行面試的工作，馬上就可以喘一口氣了。

大衛：我今天公布新的工作輪值表的時候會跟他們說。

語　法

- That is why... （那就是…的原因）

  That is why... 和 This is why... 的句型中，why 的前面都省略掉 the reason，這是口語中常見的用法，例如：*That is why* the new product sells well.（那就是新產品大賣的原因）。同樣地，也可以將 the reason why 裡的 why 省略，說成 That is the reason the new product sells well. 即可。

- help their attitude （改善他們的態度）

  help 除了有「幫助、幫忙」的字義外，還有「治療」疾病、「緩和」疼痛、「改善」事情狀況等的意思。例如當我們拿藥給一位頭痛欲裂的朋友時，可以說：This will *help* your headache.（這對紓解你的頭痛有幫助）。其他例句如：That won't *help* the situation.（那樣於事無補），Crying won't *help*.（哭也沒有用）。

Speaking Function 2

感到失望的說法

請聽《Track 13》。

1. A: We ran the advertisement for two weeks, didn't we?

   B: Yes, but I'm disappointed in the responses.

2. A: I was disappointed to hear that she wasn't coming to the party.

B: Well, she has to be in New York on that day, doesn't she?

3. A: I'm very sorry, but the trip was canceled because there weren't enough bookings.

B: That's very disappointing. I've been looking forward to it.

解說

● 要表達「失望」的心情，可以用 disappointed 這個字。「我很失望」就說 I'm disappointed。若要接續受詞、說明對某事物感到失望時，則必須先接介系詞 in, with, at, about, by 等，例如下列用法：disappointed in the decision（決定）/ disappointed with the result（結果）/ disappointed at not being invited（沒被招待）/ disappointed about not being able to go（不能去）/ disappointed by the movie（電影）。

● 另外，disappointed 還可以接續不定詞 to 表示引起失望的原因，在 to 之後通常接 hear, learn, see, find 等動詞，例如：I'm very disappointed to hear that.（我聽到那件事後非常沮喪）/ I was disappointed to learn that the project was discontinued.（當我知道計畫中止時很失望）。

● 可以順便熟悉「disappointed + that 子句」的構句方式，擴充該字的用法，例如：I'm disappointed (that) you're not coming to my birthday party.（你不能參加我的生日派對，我很失望）。

● 若要描述某件事是「令人失望的」「令人遺憾的」，留意不可用 disappointed 而必須用 disappointing 表達，例如：That's disappointing.。當然，我們也可以改用以下的說法：That's a great disappointment. / That's a real letdown. / What a disappointment! / What a pity!。

練習 1【代換】

① 請隨《Track 14》做代換練習。

1. I'm disappointed *in the decision the boss made.*
   with the result.
   at not being invited to the party.
   about not being able to go to the concert.

2. I was disappointed *to hear that she wasn't coming.*
   to learn that he didn't get promoted.
   to see him idle all day.
   to find that the store was closed.

3. I'm disappointed *you're not coming.*
   I didn't get an invitation.
   I wasn't chosen.
   I wasn't promoted.

4. "Sorry, but the balloon tour was canceled because of the strong wind."
   "That's very disappointing."
   "That's a great disappointment."
   "That's a real letdown."
   "What a disappointment!"

練習 2【角色扮演】

請隨《Track 15》在嗶一聲後唸出灰色部分的句子。

1. A: Did you reach a decision at yesterday's meeting?

   B: Yes, but I'm disappointed in the decision.

2 A: I was disappointed to hear that her first album didn't sell well.

   B: Well, let's hope her second album will sell a million copies.

3 A: I'm sorry, but the sunset cruise was canceled because of the bad weather.

   B: That's very disappointing. I've been looking forward to it.

練習 3【覆誦重要語句】

請隨《Track 16》覆誦英文句子。

1. not know how 「不知該怎麼辦」

   ↳ I don't know how to interpret what he said.
   （我不知道該如何解讀他說的話。）

2. function 「運行；起作用」

   ↳ Bureaucracies do not function efficiently.
   （官僚制度在運作上沒有效率。）

3. so far 「到目前為止」

   ↳ Three million dollars have been donated so far.
   （目前的捐款共有 300 萬美元。）

4. That is why... 「那就是…的原因；所以才…」

   ↳ That is why we decided to break off business connections with the firm.

（所以我們才決定和那家公司斷絕商業往來。）

5. frustrated 「氣餒的，沮喪的」
   ↳ The manager is quite frustrated by the low morale of the entry-level workers.
   （經理因基層員工士氣低落而感到相當氣餒。）

6. regardless of 「不管；不顧」
   ↳ Everyone, regardless of nationality, religion or sect, is welcome to participate.
   （不論國籍、宗教、黨派為何，都歡迎加入。）

7. expertise 「專門的技術，專門的知識」
   ↳ His marketing expertise will be of great help to us.
   （他的行銷專長將對我們大有幫助。）

8. at this point 「現在，此刻」
   ↳ I cannot say anything regarding the planned merger at this point.
   （在這個時候，我不便對計畫中的合併案發表看法。）

9. threaten 「威脅」
   ↳ The hijacker threatened to blow up the plane if his demands were not met.
   （劫機者揚言，若是沒達成他的要求就要炸毀飛機。）

10. be aware of 「察覺到，知道」
    ↳ He is not aware of the risks involved in starting a business of his own.（他不知道自行創業所涵蓋的風險。）

實力測驗

最近幾個月，你的公司不斷地在討論要不要擴展在中國市場的業務，而隸屬國外發展部門的你則極力主張應該把握時機。今天一早，你的上司對你說：Well, they finally decided not to expand business to China.，請你用三種不同的說法表達內心的遺憾。

參考解答

1. That's very disappointing.
2. That's a great disappointment.
3. What a disappointment!

Chapter 3

"Lite" Foods　　低卡食品

Listening

Warm-up / Pre-questions

 請聽《Track 17》的廣告後回答下面問題。

> 這段廣告特別推薦哪一種蔬菜?
> (A) 蕃茄
> (B) 玉米
> (C) 黃瓜

內容　Marjorie's Marketplace is brimming with summer color. We have the freshest fruits and vegetables to make your summer meals spectacular. Best of all, our prices are incredible—look what one dollar will buy! Our showy red tomatoes are 2 pounds for only a dollar. You can get 6 ears of sweet yellow corn for a dollar as well. Tender green broccoli crowns are 2 pounds for one dollar. Peaches and nectarines are 77 cents a pound. Pink, juicy watermelons are only 12 cents a pound!

Our recipe-featured vegetable of the week is the cool cucumber offered at 6 for only one dollar. There is nothing more refreshing than a plate of sliced cucumbers, lightly salted, and splashed with vinegar on a hot summer day. Be sure to pick up your free copy of our cool cucumber recipes at the produce counter. Marjorie's Marketplace—always making your meals easier.

中譯　　瑪佳莉超市現正洋溢著夏日的五光十色，我們提供最新鮮的蔬果，豐富您的夏日美食，而且更有您意想不到的超值特價，一塊錢就能買到最多的商品！鮮嫩的大紅蕃茄兩磅一塊錢，六根香甜的金黃玉米也只要一塊錢，淡綠色的花椰菜兩磅一塊錢，桃子和油桃都是一磅 77 分錢，粉嫩多汁的西瓜每磅則只要 12 分錢！

本週蔬菜食譜特別介紹清涼退火的黃瓜，六條只要一塊錢。炎炎夏日，來一盤稍微用鹽醃製的黃瓜切片，再淋上一點醋，有什麼東西比這來得更消暑呢？別忘了到農產品櫃檯索取一份免費的清涼黃瓜食譜。瑪佳莉超市，讓您吃得更方便。

解答　　(C)

解說　　玉米的量詞是用 ear 數，如 a ear of corn, two ears of corn；萵苣和包心菜則用 head 數，如 a head of lettuce/cabbage, two heads of lettuce/cabbage。其他字義：brim「充滿」、spectacular「豪華的」、incredible「難以相信的」、showy「艷麗的」、recipe-featured「食譜強力推薦的」、cucumber「黃瓜」、refreshing「清涼的」、splash「濺，潑」、vinegar「醋」，the produce counter 則為「農產品專櫃」之意。

Listening Step 1

 請聽《Track 18》的會話後回答下面問題。

Carol 關心什麼事？

　(A) 如何節食

　(B) 如何做菜

　(C) 如何減少糖分的攝取量

解答 (A)

Listening Step 2

熟悉下列關鍵字

chocolate-filled　裝滿巧克力的

cream puff　奶油泡芙

weakness　偏愛；極喜歡之物

split　分享；平分

strict　嚴格的

lite　低卡的

diet　節食

bathing suit　泳裝

willpower　意志力

weight　體重

pasta　義大利麵類食品

great price　物超所值

a great deal　實惠，划算

cantaloupe　洋香瓜

feature　以～為特色

specific　特定的

recipe book　食譜

light　低卡的

low-fat　低脂的

dilled　添加蒔蘿香料的

tuna　鮪魚

basil　羅勒（一種用來調味的香料植物），九層塔

spread　塗抹在麵包上的東西（如奶油、果醬等）

chilled　冷凍的

chickpea　山藜豆（或名雞豆、鷹嘴豆）

stuff　填塞（餡料）

pita　圓麵餅（中東地區的扁圓形餅）

cost effective　（錢）花得有效益的；經濟的
wholehearted support　衷心的支持
convince　說服

 請聽《Track 19》並在括弧內填入正確答案。

1. What do you say we get one of the big ones and (　　　) it?

2. I'm going to the (　　　) section for some fresh fruits and vegetables.

3. This is really a great (　　　)—three cantaloupes for only a dollar!

4. You have my (　　　　　) support on your new diet.

5. You have even (　　　) me to try to eat healthier.

解答

1. What do you say we get one of the big ones and (split) it?

2. I'm going to the (produce) section for some fresh fruits and vegetables.

3. This is really a great (deal)—three cantaloupes for only a dollar!

4. You have my (wholehearted) support on your new diet.

5. You have even (convinced) me to try to eat healthier.

 請再聽一次《Track 18》的會話後回答下面問題。

1. Molly 慫恿 Carol 一起買什麼東西吃？

　(A) 巧克力

　(B) 奶油泡芙

　(C) 洋香瓜

2. 1 美元可以買多少個洋香瓜？

　(A) 兩個

(B) 三個

(C) 五個

解答 1. (B)　2. (B)

Listening Step 3

熟悉下列語句

What do you say...?　你覺得…怎樣？

fit into　擠進

tag along　緊跟

consist of　由～組成

stick with　堅持

Good for you.　做得對。

1 請聽《Track 20》並在括弧內填入正確答案。

1. I want to lose 15 pounds by August so I can (　　)
   (　　) my bathing suit.

2. I'll (　　) (　　) with you.

3. My diet mostly (　　) (　　) fresh fruits and vegetables
   and pasta or rice.

4. I know that you can (　　) (　　) (　　).

5. (　　) (　　) (　　), Molly.

解答

1. I want to lose 15 pounds by August so I can (fit) (into) my bathing suit.

2. I'll (tag) (along) with you.

3. My diet mostly (consists) (of) fresh fruits and vegetables and pasta or

rice.

4. I know that you can (stick) (with) (it).

5. (Good) (for) (you), Molly.

 請再聽一次《Track 18》的會話後回答下面問題。

1. Carol 為什麼想節食?
   (A) 因為想變得漂亮
   (B) 為了能穿得下泳衣
   (C) 因為本身太胖了

2. Carol 為什麼喜歡到瑪佳莉超市?
   (A) 除了東西便宜之外,種類也齊全
   (B) 蔬菜水果很新鮮,又有示範如何做菜
   (C) 新鮮的農產品賣得很便宜

3. Molly 如何處理手邊的奶油泡芙?
   (A) 打算一個人全吃完
   (B) 放回原來的地方
   (C) 買回去當晚餐的點心

解答   1. (B)   2. (C)   3. (B)

Speaking

會話

 請再聽一次《Track 18》。

Molly: Oh my, Carol! Don't these chocolate-filled cream puffs look great?

Carol: They sure do! Chocolate is my major weakness in life. I love it!

Molly: What do you say we get one of the big ones and split it?

Carol: No, Molly. No thanks. I'm on a really strict, "lite" food diet. I want to lose 15 pounds by August so I can fit into my bathing suit.

Molly: What willpower you have! That's much better than I could do! I only wish I could do as well! I'm going to buy a small cream puff and eat it by myself.

Carol: You go ahead, Molly. You don't need to lose as much weight as I do anyway. I'm going to the produce section for some fresh fruits and vegetables.

Molly: Okay, I'll tag along with you. I'd like to see what your new diet consists of. Maybe I'll try it myself.

(*They go to the produce section of the supermarket.*)

Carol: My diet mostly consists of fresh fruits and vegetables and pasta or rice. I love coming to Marjorie's Marketplace because they have great prices on fresh produce.

Molly: Wow! This is a really great deal—three cantaloupes for only a dollar!

Carol: Yes, in addition to having great prices, they feature a specific fruit or vegetable each week and give away a free recipe book on various ways to cook it—usually light, low-fat recipes. This week's feature is the cucumber.

Molly: (*picking up the recipe book*) These sound delicious—

dilled tuna cucumber salad, cucumber and basil spread, chilled cucumber soup, and chickpea and cucumber stuffed pita. Ummmmmm!

Carol: Marjorie's Marketplace makes it cost effective and easy to stay on my new healthy diet.

Molly: Carol, you have my wholehearted support on your new diet. I know that you can stick with it. You have even convinced me to try to eat healthier. I'm going to put this cream puff back and buy cucumbers and cantaloupes instead.

Carol: Good for you, Molly.

中　譯 ....

茉莉：哇，卡蘿妳看！這些包巧克力的奶油泡芙看起來很好吃對不對？

卡蘿：真的耶！巧克力是我的最愛，我超喜歡吃的！

茉莉：我們合買一個大的再一人一半，好不好？

卡蘿：不要啦，謝謝妳的好意。我現在正在嚴格節食當中，只吃低卡的食物。我要在八月之前瘦下十五磅，這樣才能穿得下我的泳裝。

茉莉：妳還真能克制啊！我就沒辦法像妳那樣！真希望我也辦得到！看來我只好買一個小的奶油泡芙自己吃了。

卡蘿：買吧，反正妳不必像我要減掉那麼多的體重。我要去農產品部門買點新鮮蔬果了。

茉莉：好吧，我跟妳一塊去。我想看看妳最新的節食方法是什麼，也許我也可以自己試試。

（她們走到超市的農產品部門）

卡蘿：我主要就是靠新鮮的蔬菜水果、外加麵條或米飯來節食。我喜歡來瑪佳莉超市就是因為他們的農產品新鮮且價格都很實惠。

茉莉：哇！真的是買到賺到，三個洋香瓜只要一塊耶！

卡蘿：對啊，除了價格實惠沒話說之外，他們每週還主打一種水果或蔬菜，並發放免費食譜，裡頭有各種的烹飪方法，通常都是低熱量、低脂食物的食譜。本週強力推薦的是黃瓜。

茉莉：(拿起食譜) 看起來都好好吃喔。蒔蘿鮪魚黃瓜沙拉、抹上羅勒醬的黃瓜、冰鎮黃瓜湯、還有山藜豆黃瓜餡圓麵餅，嗯……！

卡蘿：瑪佳莉超市讓每一分錢都花得很實在，也很方便我繼續最新的健康節食計畫。

茉莉：卡蘿，我衷心支持妳的節食計畫，妳一定能堅持到底的。妳說得連我都想吃得更健康了。我要把這個奶油泡芙放回去，改買黃瓜和香瓜。

卡蘿：茉莉，妳做得很對。

語 法

● What do you say...?　（你覺得…怎樣?）

這是勸誘對方一起做某事的用法，例如：*What do you say* to a glass of beer?（來杯啤酒怎麼樣?）/ *What do you say* to going to the beach this weekend?（這個週末去海邊怎麼樣?）/ *What do you say* we take a vacation in Italy?（我們去義大利度假好不好?）。

● lite　（低卡的，低熱量的）

與 light 同義，經常被用作商品之類的名稱。

● a great deal　（實惠，划算）

deal 是「交易」「協議」之意，a great/good deal 就是指「一筆好的交

易」，相當於中文裡的「實惠」「划算」。另外，若當作習慣用法的片語時，則有「大量」「很多」的意思，例如：He knows *a great deal* about the Chinese market.（他對中國市場瞭解甚深）/ We need *a great deal* of cash.（我們需要大量的現金）。

● Good for you.　（做得對。）
這是用來讚賞對方所做的決定或行為的慣用語。

Speaking Function 3

表達鼓勵的說法

請聽《Track 21》。

1. A: Oops! I erased the data again. I don't think I'll ever learn to use this database software.

　B: You're doing fine!

2. A: I don't think I can ever finish this report.

　B: Yes, you can. You have my wholehearted support.

3. A: I'm so tired. I don't think I can ever reach the mountain top.

　B: Stick to it!

解說

● 對於剛開始起步、但因事情無法順利進展而漸失信心的人，我們可以對他說：You're doing fine! / You're doing very well! / You're doing great!，鼓勵他重拾信心。另外，也可以拿自己跟對方做比較，自我調侃地說出 That's better than I could do.（你比我好多了）或 I wish I could do as well.（真希望我也能做到像你那樣）來安慰對方。

● 對於深感煩惱的人，我們可以用 support 和 backing（支持）等字

來安慰鼓勵，例如 You have my wholehearted support. 和 You have my backing. 等的說法。若用片語表達，可以說成 I'm right behind you. / I stand by you.（我支持你）。

● 在比賽等場合中，我們會大喊「加油!」來為選手或對方打氣，換成英文則是說成 Stick to it! / Come on! / Go on! / Keep it up! 等，都是將「衷心希望對方拼出全力得到好成績」的心情傳達給對方知道。

練習 1【代換】

 請隨《Track 22》做代換練習。

1. "Oops! I pressed the wrong key. I don't think I'll ever learn to touch-type."
   "*You're doing fine!*"
   "You're doing very well!"
   "You're doing great!"
   "That's better than I could do."

2. "I don't think I can run the store properly anymore."
   "*Yes, you can. You have my wholehearted support.*"
   "Yes, you can. You have my backing."
   "Yes, you can. I'm right behind you."
   "Yes, you can. I stand by you."

3. "My legs are hurting. I don't think I can keep running this hard to reach the goal."
   "*Stick to it!*"
   "Come on!"
   "Go on!"

"Keep it up!"

"Keep at it!"

練習 2 【角色扮演】

① 請隨《Track 23》在嗶一聲後唸出灰色部分的句子。

1. A: Ouch! I didn't realize snowboarding was so difficult. I don't think I'll ever learn.

   B: You're doing fine!

2. A: I don't think I can ever finish this project.

   B: Yes, you can. You have my wholehearted support.

3. A: I'm a lousy tennis player. I can't hit the ball right.

   B: Stick to it!

練習 3 【覆誦重要語句】

① 請隨《Track 24》覆誦英文句子。

1. weakness 「偏愛；極喜歡之物」

   ↳ She has a weakness for chocolate. (她很喜歡吃巧克力。)

2. What do you say...? 「你覺得…怎樣?」

   ↳ What do you say we scuba dive in the Caribbean?
   (我們到加勒比海潛水怎麼樣?)

3. willpower 「意志力」

   ↳ I don't think he has willpower strong enough to quit smoking. (我不認為他的意志力足以使他戒菸成功。)

4. lose weight 「減輕體重」

   ↳ I lost weight on a diet and then gained it back.
   (我節食後體重有減輕，但後來又胖回來了。)

5. tag along 「緊跟」
  ↳ Whenever I go shopping she always tags along.
  （我每次去購物，她都會跟來。）

6. consist of 「由～組成」
  ↳ The United Nations Security Council consists of five permanent members and ten non-permanent members.
  （聯合國安理會是由五個常任理事國以及十個非常任理事國所組成。）

7. a great deal 「實惠，划算」
  ↳ Three CDs for twenty dollars is a great deal.
  （三片 CD 才 20 美元，實在太划算了。）

8. feature 「以～為特色，特別介紹」
  ↳ This week's Time magazine features American teenagers.
  （本週《時代》雜誌針對美國青少年作了專題報導。）

9. wholehearted 「衷心的」
  ↳ I received his wholehearted support to attain this goal.
  （他誠心祝福我能達成目標。）

10. stick with 「堅持」
  ↳ Stick with it and you'll succeed in the end.
  （堅持到最後，成功就是屬於你的。）

實力測驗

同事 Tom 正利用 PowerPoint 準備商品發表會，但因不擅長運用而使得效果不佳，對此他非常沮喪。請用三種不同的說法來為他加油打氣。

參考解答

1. You're doing fine!
2. That's better than I could do.
3. Keep at it.

Chapter 4	**Negotiating**	交　涉

Listening

Warm-up / Pre-questions

 請聽《Track 25》的新聞報導後回答下面問題。

紙的價格為什麼會上漲？
  (A) 因為匯率變動
  (B) 因為製紙工廠減少
  (C) 因為紙的原料價格上漲

內容　Small businesses are being hit hard as suppliers and distributors of paper products increase prices across the board. All small businesses, regardless of the type, require paper products to function—envelopes, letterhead, business cards, invoices, and the like. A monthly budget of $500 for paper type products is now about $650. This increase can make or break a struggling business over the long haul.

Paper prices have shot up in recent months because there are too few facilities to meet the heavy demand. In the last five years many paper factories have shut down because they were capital-intensive and difficult to run profitably. Now, without enough factories to produce paper products to meet the demand, factory margins are rising and are likely to keep doing so for several years.

中譯　紙類產品的供應商和經銷商全面漲價，使得中小企業大受打擊。

不論何種類型的中小企業都需要紙張才能運作，舉凡信封、印有信頭的信紙、名片、發票等都需要紙張。原本一個月 500 美元預算的紙張費用，現在調漲為 650 美元左右。長期下來，這項額外的支出可能會決定一家倒閉邊緣的企業是否存活。

最近幾個月的紙價暴漲，原因是生產設備不足，造成供不應求的現象。由於造紙業需要大量資金，再加上難以賺取利潤，所以過去五年來，有許多工廠關門大吉。如今紙張供不應求，剩下不多的工廠獲利相對增加，而且這種榮景可望持續好幾年。

解答　(B)

解說　進行式的被動語態是「be 動詞 + being + 過去分詞」，而上面短文中 Small businesses are being hit hard... 是指「中小企業受到嚴重的打擊」。單字的意思如下：small businesses「中小企業」、hit「給與打擊」、hard「嚴重地」、supplier「供應商」、distributor「經銷商」、paper product「紙製品」、across the board「全面地」、letterhead「上端印有公司名、地址、電話等的信紙」、budget「預算」、paper type products「紙類製品」、make or break「左右命運」、struggle「掙扎」、over the long haul「長期下來，結果」、shoot up「暴漲」、meet「滿足」、demand「需求」、shut down「關閉」、capital-intensive「資本密集的」、profitably「有利地」，而 margin 為「利潤，成本與售價之間的差額」之意。

Listening Step 1

 請聽《Track 26》的會話後回答下面問題。

Michael 和供應商正在討論什麼問題？
　(A) 進貨量
　(B) 進貨日期

(C) 大量進貨的價格折扣

解答　　　　　　　　　　　　　　　　　　　　　　　(C)

Listening Step 2

熟悉下列關鍵字

---

supply　供應品; 存貨

warehouse　倉庫

indicate　指出

across-the-board　全面的

price increase　價格上揚

minimize　使減到最小

volume discount　數量折扣（對於大宗購買所給予的折扣）

raise　提高

approximately　大概

significant　顯著的, 相當的

maximum　最大量

purchase　購買

---

①請聽《Track 27》並在括弧內填入正確答案。

1. My boss just received your notice (　　　) an across-the-board price increase for all of your products.

2. He was hoping to make some kind of arrangement with you to (　　　) the price increases.

3. Well, my boss was wondering, since we buy so many products, if you could possibly give us a (　　　) discount?

4. That's a (　　　　) discount.

5. 15% is our (　　　　).

解答

1. My boss just received your notice (indicating) an across-the-board price increase for all of your products.

2. He was hoping to make some kind of arrangement with you to (minimize) the price increases.

3. Well, my boss was wondering, since we buy so many products, if you could possibly give us a (volume) discount?

4. That's a (significant) discount.

5. 15% is our (maximum).

1 請再聽一次《Track 26》的會話後回答下面問題。

1. Michael 的老闆收到了什麼?

(A) 通知單

(B) 請款單

(C) 產品折扣價目表

2. Michael 要求給予多少的折扣?

(A) 15 %

(B) 18 %

(C) 20 %

解答　　　　　　　　　　　　　　　　1. (A)　2. (C)

Listening Step 3

熟悉下列語句

```
give ～ a call    打電話給（人）
see if...    看看是否…
work out    想出
some kind of    某種的
be open to    敞開心胸去，樂意於接受
ask for    要求
on balances    交付尾款，結清（買方先賒帳取貨，至結算日才付清貨款的
交易方式）
```

1 請聽《Track 28》並在括弧內填入正確答案。

1. Well, my boss asked me to give you a call and see if we could (   ) (   ) an arrangement for the purchase of our supplies from your warehouse.

2. He was hoping to make (   ) (   ) (   ) arrangement with you to minimize the price increases.

3. I'm (   ) (   ) hearing what you're interested in doing.

4. He told me to (   ) (   ) a 20% volume discount.

5. How about if we give you a 15% discount (   ) (   ) paid within 30 days?

解答

1. Well, my boss asked me to give you a call and see if we could (work) (out) an arrangement for the purchase of our supplies from your warehouse.

2. He was hoping to make (some) (kind) (of) arrangement with you to

minimize the price increases.

3. I'm (open) (to) hearing what you're interested in doing.

4. He told me to (ask) (for) a 20% volume discount.

5. How about if we give you a 15% discount (on) (balances) paid within 30 days?

 請再聽一次《Track 26》的會話後回答下面問題。

1. Michael 為什麼打電話給 Mr. Sanders？
   (A) 因為想起重要的事
   (B) 因為老闆交代他打電話
   (C) 因為之前約好要打電話聯絡

2. Michael 為什麼會要求給予一些折扣？
   (A) 因為他和對方的老闆是好朋友
   (B) 因為他是該供應商的最大客戶
   (C) 因為他公司的貨品幾乎全都是跟該供應商所購買

3. Michael 聽完 Mr.Sanders 的回答之後有什麼看法？
   (A) 覺得老闆一定會很高興
   (B) 不甚滿意
   (C) 自己覺得還好，但老闆一定不滿意

解答   1. (B)   2. (C)   3. (A)

Speaking

會話

 請再聽一次《Track 26》。

Michael: Hi, Mr. Sanders. This is Michael from Quick Copy.

Mr. Sanders: Oh, hi, Michael. What can we get for you this week?

Michael: Well, my boss asked me to give you a call and see if we could work out an arrangement for the purchase of our supplies from your warehouse.

Mr. Sanders: What do you mean, Michael?

Michael: My boss just received your notice indicating an across-the-board price increase for all of your products. Since we buy almost all of our products and supplies from your company, he was hoping to make some kind of arrangement with you to minimize the price increases.

Mr. Sanders: Your company is a very good customer of ours, so I'm open to hearing what you're interested in doing.

Michael: Well, my boss was wondering, since we buy so many products, if you could possibly give us a volume discount?

Mr. Sanders: What kind of discount was he looking for?

Michael: He told me to ask for a 20% volume discount since you've raised prices approximately 20%.

Mr. Sanders: That's a significant discount. We don't usually give discounts like that. 15% is our maximum.

Michael: What can you do for us then?

Mr. Sanders: How about if we give you a 15% discount on balances paid within 30 days and an 18% discount on all cash purchases?

Michael: That sounds pretty good. My boss will be happy to hear this. Thanks for helping us. We'd like to continue to be one of your best customers.

中　譯 ....

麥　可：山德斯先生您好，我是快印公司的麥可。

山德斯：喔，麥可你好，我們這禮拜要幫你們準備什麼？

麥　可：嗯，我的老闆要我打個電話給你，看我們是不是能就進貨的交易細節討論一下。

山德斯：麥可，你的意思是……？

麥　可：我們老闆剛才收到通知說貴公司的產品將全面漲價，因為我們的所有紙類製品和供應品幾乎都是向貴公司購買的，所以他希望能和你們磋商，將價格的漲幅降到最低。

山德斯：貴公司是我們非常優良的客戶，所以我很樂意聽聽看你們的想法。

麥　可：我們老闆的意思是，既然我們買的產品的量這麼大，是不是有可能給我們一些折扣？

山德斯：他想要怎樣的折扣？

麥　可：因為你們把價格調漲了 20% 左右，他要我向你們爭取 20% 的折扣。

山德斯：那可是很大的折扣啊。我們通常不給那種折扣的，15% 是我們的上限。

麥　可：那你們能提供怎樣的優惠?

山德斯：三十天內付清的話,給你們 15% 的折扣,如果全部付現,
　　　　就給你們 18% 的折扣,你覺得怎麼樣?

麥　可：聽起來很不錯,我老闆聽了一定很高興。謝謝你們的幫
　　　　忙,我們會一直是你們最好的客戶。

語　法 ....

● give you a call　(打電話給你)

「打電話」通常會使用 call, call up, telephone, phone 等字,順便也可
以記下「give + 人 + a call」的用法,例如 I'll *give you a call* later.(我
等一下打電話給你)。另外,「我再打電話給你」除了 I'll call you again.
之外,也經常使用 I'll call you back. 的說法。

● almost all of　(幾乎所有的)

almost all of our product 可以省略 of,變成 almost all our product, 但
切記不可再省略 all,這是因為 almost 通常不直接修飾名詞。

● How about if...　(…怎麼樣?)

How about... 是邀請和提議的句型,後面通常接續名詞或動名詞,不
過也可以如會話中的句子,接續 if 子句,其他例句如: *How about if
we take his car?* (我們搭他的便車怎麼樣?)。

Speaking Function 4

能與不能的說法

請聽《Track 29》。

1. A: Can you reduce the price?

　 B: Yes. I can give you a ten percent discount.

2. A: The knob came off.

   B: I can fix it.

3. A: Can you double the profit?

   B: I'm not sure I can.

解說

● 直接詢問對方「能～嗎?」的基本句型是 Can you ～? 和 Are you able to ～? 這兩種，尤其以前者的使用頻率最高。Could you ～? 則比 Can you ～? 來得更有禮貌。另外，間接詢問對方的用法為 I wonder if you can ～. 和 Do you think you can ～? 等。

● I can ～ 和 I'm able to ～ 是直接表達自己「能」做某事的句型；間接的表達方式是 I think I can ～。若無法確信能夠做到時，可以說 I might be able to ～，而 I'd say I'm able to ～ 則為委婉的說法。

● 要表達「無法，不能」時，使用 I can't ～；間接句則為 I'm not sure I can ～ 和 I don't think I can ～ / I don't feel able to ～。至於 I wouldn't say I'm able to ～ 則為其委婉的說法。若要強烈表達「根本不可能」，可以使用 I can't possibly ～ 或 There's no way I can ～ 等的說法。

練習 1 【代換】

 請隨《Track 30》做代換練習。

  1. *Can you*   make out the invoice by noon?

     Could you

     Do you think you can

     Are you able to

     I wonder if you can

2. *I can*   settle the dispute.

> I think I can
> I'm able to
> I might be able to
> I'd say I'm able to

3. *I'm not sure I can*   manage the project.

> I don't think I can
> I can't possibly
> There's no way I can
> I don't feel able to
> I wouldn't say I'm able to

練習 2【角色扮演】

 請隨《Track 31》在嗶一聲後唸出灰色部分的句子。

1. A: Can you cut the costs?

   B: I think I can.

2. A: What can we do with those angry customers?

   B: I can handle them.

3. A: Can you deliver it to us tomorrow?

   B: I'm not sure we can.

練習 3【覆誦重要語句】

 請隨《Track 32》覆誦英文句子。

1. give ～ a call 「打電話給（人）」

   ↳ I'll give you a call as soon as I get out of work.

   （我一下班就打電話給你。）

2. see if... 「看看是否…」

↳ Will you see if they are interested in doing the project with us?

（可否請你確認他們是不是有意跟我們合作這個計畫?）

3. work out 「想出」

↳ After several meetings we could finally work out a set of compromises for the proposal.（幾次開會下來，我們好不容易才想出這個計畫的折衷方案。）

4. indicate 「指出」

↳ New research indicates that eating breakfast can reduce the effects of stress.

（最新研究指出，吃早餐能減輕壓力帶來的影響。）

5. some kind of 「某種的」

↳ Eight of ten restaurants in Los Angeles offer some kind of ethnic dishes.（洛杉磯的餐館中，十家有八家賣的都是某一國風味的料理。）

6. minimize 「使減到最小」

↳ We have to think of ways to minimize the risks.
（我們得想些方法把風險降到最低。）

7. be open to 「敞開心胸去，樂意於接受」

↳ We're always open to our customers' suggestions.
（我們都很歡迎顧客的建議。）

8. ask for 「要求」

↳ A number of people came here to ask for copies of the new catalog.（很多人來這裡索取新的目錄。）

9. significant 「顯著的，相當的」

↳There has been significant change in consumer preferences in the past five years.

（過去五年來，顧客的喜好有明顯的改變。）

10. maximum 「最大量；最大的」

↳We are making maximum efforts to recycle our office supplies.

（我們盡最大的努力來進行辦公用品的資源回收。）

實力測驗

有一天，公司的總經理當面吩咐你一個月內提出 e-business（電子商務）的企劃案來。你心裡想著「嗯，真難。」你要如何說出自己的看法呢？請以三種不同的說法表達。

參考解答　　1. It seems impossible, but I'd say I'm able to do it.

2. I can't possibly do it in such a short period of time.

3. I wouldn't say I'm able to do it in a month.

Chapter 5

Companion Animals

動物——
您的最佳拍檔

Listening

Warm-up / Pre-questions

 請聽《Track 33》的廣告後回答下面問題。

禮拜六在哈里遜路上的寵物公司將舉辦什麼活動?

(A) 寵物拍賣會

(B) 貓狗服裝秀

(C) 等待領養的動物展示會

內容　Have you ever considered getting a pet? There are many adorable pets just waiting to be adopted by the right person. The Ralph Jones Animal Shelter will be showcasing many of its pets that are available for adoption this Saturday at The Pet Company on Harrison Road.

Stop by between 11 a.m. and 4 p.m. and find the companion animal of your dreams. There are cats and dogs of every age and every breed available. There are even pure breeds ready for adoption. You can take your pet home the same day. A pet needs you and you need a companion animal. See you Saturday.

中譯　您曾想過要養隻寵物嗎? 有很多可愛的寵物正等著合適的主人來領養。本週六拉夫·瓊斯動物收容所將在哈里遜路上的寵物公司展示許多的寵物供您認養。

歡迎於早上 11 點到下午 4 點前來挑選最理想的寵物作伴。現場

有各種年齡、各種品種的貓狗可供領養，甚至還有純種的喔！
當天您就可以把寵物帶回家。寵物需要您，而您也需一隻寵物
作伴。星期六見囉！

解答 (C)

解說 consider + V.ing 是「考慮做～」的意思；由於 consider 不可接
不定詞做受詞，所以不能用 consider to do。adopt 原本指「收養
子女」，現在也可以指「收養寵物」。animal shelter 即「動物收
容所、流浪動物之家」，專門收養被人類遺棄的動物。companion
animal 是現今美國廣泛使用的詞彙，特指不將動物單純視為寵
物（被人類豢養的動物），而是視之為人類最好的同伴。其他字
義：adorable「可愛的」、showcase「展示」、adoption「收養」、
stop by「順便到」、breed「品種」、available「可得到的」，而 pure
breed 為「純種」之意。

Listening Step 1

 請聽《Track 34》的會話後回答下面問題。

這位女士想要領養什麼樣的狗？

(A) 小型犬

(B) 忠實的狗

(C) 會看家的狗

解答   (A)

Listening Step 2

熟悉下列關鍵字

cocker spaniel   可卡長耳獵犬

poodle　貴賓狗

terrier　㹴犬（打獵或玩賞用的小型狗）

work　起作用；行得通

female　雌的

male　雄的

spunky　有精神的

personality　個性

well-behaved　守規矩的

housebroken　（貓、狗等）經過訓練而有居家衛生習慣的

loyal　忠心的

former　從前的

owner　飼主

quarantine　檢疫

cage　（鳥、獸）籠

① 請聽《Track 35》並在括弧內填入正確答案。

1. She is a beautiful poodle with a (　　　) personality.

2. But she is very (　　　　).

3. Of course she is (　　　　　) as well.

4. She was very (　　　) to her former owner.

5. They have strict (　　　　　) laws there.

解答

1. She is a beautiful poodle with a (spunky) personality.

2. But she is very (well-behaved).

3. Of course she is (housebroken) as well.

4. She was very (loyal) to her former owner.

5. They have strict (quarantine) laws there.

(1) 請再聽一次《Track 34》的會話後回答下面問題。

1. 女士曾經在什麼時候養過可卡長耳獵犬？
   (A) 養到不久前才沒養
   (B) 在她小時候
   (C) 在她 15 歲的時候

2. Binkie 是隻什麼樣的狗？
   (A) 活力充沛、有良好衛生習慣的狗
   (B) 忠心又聽話的狗
   (C) 個性有些神經質的狗，但非常討人喜歡

解答　　　　　　　　　　　　　　　　　　1. (B)　　2. (A)

Listening Step 3

熟悉下列語句

move out　搬走，搬出去
be bound to　一定會
be partial to　偏袒；偏愛
be in the military　在軍中
put up for　拿出；公開某物徵求（認養者或買主等）
come out of　走出，從～出來

(1) 請聽《Track 36》並在括弧內填入正確答案。

1. My roommate just (　　　) (　　　) and I'm kind of lonely.

2. We have several dogs here today, one of which (　　　) (　　　) (　　　) make a good companion for you.

3. The husband was (　　　) (　　　) (　　　) and they had to move overseas to Germany.

4. They decided it was best to (　　　) Binkie (　　　)
(　　　) adoption here.

5. Can she (　　　) (　　　) (　　　) the cage for a minute to
play with me?

解答

1. My roommate just (moved) (out) and I'm kind of lonely.

2. We have several dogs here today, one of which (is) (bound) (to) make a
good companion for you.

3. The husband was (in) (the) (military) and they had to move overseas to
Germany.

4. They decided it was best to (put) Binkie (up) (for) adoption here.

5. Can she (come) (out) (of) the cage for a minute to play with me?

---

1 請再聽一次《Track 34》的會話後回答下面問題。

1. 女士為什麼想要領養寵物？
   (A) 因為原先飼養的寵物死了
   (B) 因為家裡的小孩想要養
   (C) 因為室友搬走後覺得很寂寞

2. 她為什麼覺得母狗比公狗好？
   (A) 母狗比較乖巧
   (B) 母狗還會生小狗
   (C) 因為她小時候養的狗是母狗

3. 以前飼養 Binkie 的主人為什麼沒帶牠一起到德國去？
   (A) 嫌帶牠一起上飛機的手續麻煩
   (B) 因為德國的檢疫法律的相關規定很嚴格
   (C) 因為德國法律規定不准在公寓內飼養寵物

Speaking

會話

請再聽一次《Track 34》。

Worker: Hi. Can we help you find a pet for adoption today?

Customer: Yes. I want to find a dog that would be a good companion. My roommate just moved out and I'm kind of lonely.

Worker: Oh, I am sorry to hear about your roommate. I think we can find you a nice animal friend, though. We have several dogs here today, one of which is bound to make a good companion for you.

Customer: I want a small dog because I live in an apartment. I'm pretty healthy to be 67 years old so I can take the dog for a walk every day. Because of the size of my apartment, it's just easier to have a small dog.

Worker: I see. Have you ever had a dog before?

Customer: Yes, I had a cocker spaniel when I was a child. She died when I was 15. I loved that dog. She was a great companion. Sometimes she was like my best friend.

Worker: I'm sorry, but our last cocker spaniel was adopted this morning. We have two really small dogs left, though, a poodle and a terrier that might work. Would you like to see them?

Customer: Yes, I certainly would. I'm kind of partial to female dogs because our cocker spaniel was a female.

Worker: All right. The poodle is a female and the terrier is a male.

Customer: Good. Let's start by looking at the poodle, then.

Worker: This is Binkie. She is two years old. She is a beautiful poodle with a spunky personality, but she is very well-behaved. Of course she is housebroken as well. She was very loyal to her former owner so she would be a great companion to you.

Customer: She is so cute! I think she likes me already! Why did her former owner put her up for adoption?

Worker: The husband was in the military and they had to move overseas to Germany. They have strict quarantine laws there so they decided it was best to put Binkie up for adoption here.

Customer: Poor Binkie. She must be as lonely as I am without my roommate! Can she come out of the cage for a minute to play with me?

Worker: Sure.

(*After a few minutes of playing with Binkie*)

Customer: I don't need to look anymore. I think Binkie is a perfect companion for me. I will take her.

中　譯 ....

職員：您好，需要我們幫您找隻寵物來領養嗎？

顧客： 好啊，我想要找一隻狗當我的好伙伴。我的室友剛搬走，我有點寂寞。

職員： 啊，我很難過聽到您室友搬走的消息，不過我們可以幫您找隻動物作伴。今天這裡有好幾隻狗，可以選一隻來好好陪伴您。

顧客： 我住在公寓裡，所以我要一隻體型小一點的狗。我67歲了，但身體還很硬朗，每天可以帶狗去散步，只是受限於公寓的空間，養一隻小型狗比較方便。

職員： 我明白了，那您以前養過狗嗎？

顧客： 有啊，我小時候養過可卡長耳獵犬，她在我15歲的時候死了。我很喜歡那隻狗，她是很好的伙伴，有時候就像是我最好的朋友。

職員： 很抱歉，今天早上已經有人把最後一隻可卡長耳獵犬領養走了，不過還有兩隻體型很小的狗兒也許適合您，一隻是貴賓狗，另外一隻是㹴犬，您要不要看一下？

顧客： 當然好啊。我稍微比較偏愛母狗，因為我之前養的可卡長耳獵犬就是母的。

職員： 沒問題，貴賓狗是母的，㹴犬是公的。

顧客： 好，那我們先看貴賓狗吧。

職員： 這是冰琪，兩歲大，是隻很漂亮的貴賓狗，生性好動，但很守規矩，而且在家的衛生習慣很好，對以前的主人也很忠心，所以一定會是您很好的伴。

顧客： 好可愛喔！我覺得她已經喜歡上我了！她之前的主人為什麼把她送來這裡讓人領養呢？

職員： 因為男主人在軍中服務，後來得搬到德國去，而當地的檢疫法規相當嚴格，所以他們認為還是把冰琪送來這裡讓人

領養比較好。

顧客：好可憐喔，就跟我沒了室友一樣，一定很孤單！可以把她從籠子裡放出來陪我玩一下嗎？

職員：當然可以。

（和冰琪玩了幾分鐘之後）

顧客：不用再看別的了。我覺得冰琪會是我絕佳的同伴，就是她了。

語　法

● make a good companion for you　（成為你的良伴）

make 是「成為」的意思，含有「能力上及個性上都適合」的意味，例如：He will *make* a good doctor.（他會成為一位好醫生）/ She will *make* a good teacher.（她會成為一位好老師）。主詞未必限定於人，也可以使用於物，例如：This garage will *make* a good laboratory.（這個車庫將會是一間很棒的實驗室）。

● I'm pretty healthy to be 67 years old.　（以 67 歲的年紀來講，我身體還很硬朗。）

「以～年紀來講，還是…」的英語說法可以用「主詞＋be 動詞＋形容詞＋to be ＋歲數」表達，其他例句如：He is quite energetic to be 70 years old.（以 70 歲的年紀來講，他精力還很充沛）。

● that might work　（那或許有用）

work 有「順利進行」的意思，用法如以下例句：His plan *worked* well.（他的計畫進展得很順利）/ My idea didn't *work*.（我的點子不管用）/ This might *work*.（這招可能奏效）。

● be partial to　（偏袒；偏愛）

be partial to 有「偏袒」和「偏愛」兩種意思，例句如 Miss Nelson *is partial to* girl students.（尼爾森老師偏袒女學生）/ Miss Nelson *is partial to* chocolate.（尼爾森老師對巧克力有所偏好）等。

Speaking Function 5

表達希望、願望的說法

請聽《Track 37》。

1. A: I want a map of this city.

   B: You can get it at the gas station.

2. A: I'm dying for a cup of coffee.

   B: Well, there's a café around the corner. Let's go there.

3. A: I wish I were allowed to have a pet in my apartment.

   B: You might want to consider moving to an apartment where you can keep a pet.

解說

● 想要某樣東西的最基本說法是 I want～，若要說得禮貌些則是 I'd like ～。表達強烈的希望得到則是 I'd very much like ～，亦即使用 very much 來修飾。「需要」的 need 也是表希望得到的字，最簡單的用法是 I need ～，其他如 What I need is ～（我需要的是～）/ All I need is ～（我需要的只是～）。

● 表需求度高、非常想要的一般說法是 I'm dying for ～。I'm dying for a cup of coffee. 即是「我很想要喝杯咖啡」的意思，這句話還可以改用 desperate（極度渴望的）一字表達，即 I'm desperate for a cup of coffee.；或是用副詞 badly（非常地）修飾，說成 I badly need a cup of coffee.。另外，使用「必須」之意造句的 I must have ～和 I've got to have ～等，也是表達極度希望的說法。

● 對於難以實現的願望（即希望不大）的表達句型是 I wish I could ～，如 I wish I could drink wine.（真希望能喝酒）；也可以使用 If only I could ～的句型，如 If only I could drive a car.（如果我會開車就好了）。

練習 1【代換】

請隨《Track 38》做代換練習。

    1. *I want*   a copy of the convention program.

        I'd like

        I'd very much like

        I need

    2. *I'm dying for*   a cigarette.

        I'm desperate for

        I must have

        I've got to have

    3. I wish I could *drink wine.*

                  get a single room.

                  come to your party.

                  take a vacation.

練習 2【角色扮演】

請隨《Track 39》在嗶一聲後唸出灰色部分的句子。

    1. A: I want your new catalog and price list.

       B: I'll mail them to you right away.

    2. A: I'm dying for a cold drink.

       B: Well, there's a vending machine over there. Let's go and

          get one.

    3. A: You live in the suburbs, don't you?

       B: Yes, but I wish I could live closer to work.

練習 3【覆誦重要語句】

 請隨《Track 40》覆誦英文句子。

1. move out 「搬走，搬出去」
   ↳My next-door neighbor moved out of his apartment just last week. (我家隔壁的鄰居上禮拜從這間公寓搬走了。)

2. be bound to 「一定會」
   ↳The company is bound to go bankrupt sooner or later.
   (這家公司遲早一定會破產。)

3. to be ～ years old 「以～年紀來講」
   ↳He is quite lithe in build to be 60 years old.
   (以 60 歲的年紀來講，他身體還很柔軟。)

4. adopt 「收養」
   ↳The couple was not able to have a child of their own, so they decided to adopt a child.
   (這對夫婦無法生育，所以決定領養一個小孩。)

5. work 「起作用；行得通」
   ↳His suggestion sounds good, but I don't think it will work. (他的建議聽起來是不錯，但我覺得行不通。)

6. be partial to 「偏袒；偏愛」
   ↳The children think their teacher is partial to some students, especially girls. (這些小孩覺得他們的老師對某些學生偏心，特別是對女孩子。)

7. spunky 「有精神的」
   ↳Mary is as spunky and cheerful as ever.
   (瑪麗一如往常神采奕奕。)

8. well-behaved 「守規矩的」

↳All Mike's friends who came to his birthday party were well-behaved.

（所有來參加麥可生日派對的朋友都很守規矩。）

9. loyal 「忠心的」

↳Most of the fans remained loyal to the team even though they lost most of the games.（雖然這支球隊輸了大半的比賽，但大部分的球迷依然很忠誠。）

10. put up for 「拿出；公開某物徵求（認養者或買主等）」

↳We're putting our villa up for sale.

（我們正要把別墅賣掉。）

實力測驗

在一個炎炎夏日裡，你和朋友比賽打網球，但沒想到他比想像中還難以應付。為了想贏他，你不斷在場中跑來跑去，使勁揮動球拍，因此流了很多汗，而且口乾舌燥。終於可以稍事休息了，你趕緊跟朋友說：「真想喝杯水。」請用三種不同的說法表達。

參考解答

1. I'm dying for a glass of water.

2. I've got to have a glass of water.

3. I'm desperate for a glass of water.

Company Policy 公司政策

Listening

Warm-up / Pre-questions

 請聽《Track 41》的新聞報導後回答下面問題。

離職的員工以後會怎樣？
(A) 會有不利的處境
(B) 會沒有找到第二份工作的機會
(C) 會比較容易找到新的工作

內容　Companies in today's lackluster economy are requiring current and laid-off employees to abide by employment agreements. These legal agreements can cover all sorts of activities and communication. For example, they may limit a laid-off worker from joining a competitor, from derogating a former company, disclosing information gained while on the job, calling on former customers and even from calling old colleagues from work.

Employers insist that they must protect themselves from trade secret theft and retaliatory measures by angry laid-off workers. In contrast, employees are distressed by the threat of lawsuits, alienation from former customers and colleague friends, and the lost opportunities with other companies. This puts the job seeker in a precarious position—laid-off employees are often under agreement with the old company, but many new employers now want new employees to sign an agreement promising that they are not bound by any legal contracts with former employers.

中譯　在當今經濟環境不佳的情況下，企業往往要求員工，不論是在職期間或被解雇之後，都得遵守聘雇合約。這類合約規範各種活動和人際關係，例如：離職員工不得到競爭的同業公司求職、不得毀謗原公司、洩漏過去在職時獲得的資訊、不得拜訪舊客戶、甚至不得聯絡以前的同事。

雇主堅持必須保護自身，以防範心生不滿的解雇員工竊取商業機密或採取報復手段。另一方面，員工不僅飽受可能的訴訟壓力，又要疏離舊客戶和老同事，還失去在其他公司求職的機會，這使得求職者的處境相當不利──因為解雇員工通常和原公司簽了約，但現在許多新的雇主希望新員工簽約保證並不受原公司的合約限制。

解答　(A)

解說　連接詞 while 是「在～時候」的意思，可以引導從屬子句，而從內文中 while on the job 這一句子，可以看出當 while 子句的主詞與主要子句的主詞一致時，可省略「主詞（代名詞）+ be」。其他字義：lackluster「無活力的」、laid-off employee「被解雇的員工」、abide「遵守」、employment agreement「聘雇合約」、legal「法律上的」、cover「涵蓋」、competitor「競爭對手」、derogate「貶損」、disclose「使顯露」、call on「拜訪」、trade secret theft「竊取商業機密」、retaliatory measures「報復手段」、distressed「苦惱的」、threat「威脅」、lawsuit「訴訟」、alienation「疏遠」、precarious「不安定的」、bind「束縛」，而 legal contract 為「有法律效力的合約」之意。

Listening Step 1

 請聽《Track 42》的會話後回答下面問題。

Balmert 先生被要求做什麼？

  (A) 正式上班後要好好認真工作

  (B) 在規定守密、不拉攏客戶的合約上簽名

  (C) 同意每天加班及週六上班的規定

解答   (B)

Listening Step 2

熟悉下列關鍵字

paperwork　文書工作；書面作業

sales representative　業務代表；推銷員

confidentiality　保密

non-solicitation　禁止挖角（離職後不得拉攏公司客戶）

client bases　基本客戶群

pricing structure　價格結構

proprietary　（公司本身）獨占擁有的

benefit　利益

govern　支配；約束（行動等）

competitor　競爭對手

solicit　拉攏

legally　法律上；合法地

liable　有責任的

derogatory　貶損的

logic　邏輯；道理

specialty　專長

contractual　契約上的
agreement　合約
termination　終止
intellectual property　智慧財產（權）
trade secret　商業機密
designated　選定的
generous　慷慨的
severance　解僱
package　一套完整的方案（建議等）
unlikely　不太可能的
compensation　補償；補償金
recall　叫回；重新雇用
layoff　臨時解僱

① 請聽《Track 43》並在括弧內填入正確答案。

1. For a period of one year you won't be able to work with any of our (　　　　).

2. You'll be legally· (　　) if you spread derogatory information about the company.

3. I'm not quite sure I follow the (　　) behind the idea of not working for a competitor.

4. If you think about intellectual (　　) protection and trade secret theft, I'm confident you'll understand what I'm getting at.

5. You'll receive six months of salary as (　　　　).

解答
1. For a period of one year you won't be able to work with any of our

(competitors).

2. You'll be legally (liable) if you spread derogatory information about the company.

3. I'm not quite sure I follow the (logic) behind the idea of not working for a competitor.

4. If you think about intellectual (property) protection and trade secret theft, I'm confident you'll understand what I'm getting at.

5. You'll receive six months of salary as (compensation).

1 請再聽一次《Track 42》的會話後回答下面問題。

1. 對於合約，Balmert 有哪一點不清楚？
   (A) 公司的薪資體系和升遷制度
   (B) 合約本身的全部內容
   (C) 合約內容會對自己帶來什麼直接的影響

2. Balmert 若在簽約後中途離職或被炒魷魚，將被合約限定幾年內不得到競爭的同行工作？
   (A) 半年
   (B) 一年
   (C) 兩年

解答   1. (C)   2. (B)

Listening Step 3

熟悉下列語句

go over   察看；檢查
get through   完成
get started   開始

be familiar with　熟悉

to a certain degree　某種程度上

call on　拜訪

get at　意指

It's hard to say.　這很難說。

① 請聽《Track 44》並在括弧內填入正確答案。

1. I'm glad that we could get together to (　　) (　　) a few documents before you start your new position here at Franklin, Inc.

2. Well, let's (　　) (　　) this paperwork so that you can get started on your real job as a sales representative here.

3. Yes, (　　) (　　) (　　) (　　).

4. You won't be able to (　　) (　　) or solicit from any of our clients.

5. I'm confident that you'll understand what I'm (　　) (　　).

解答

1. I'm glad that we could get together to (go) (over) a few documents before you start your new position here at Franklin, Inc.

2. Well, let's (get) (through) this paperwork so that you can get started on your real job as a sales representative here.

3. Yes, (to) (a) (certain) (degree).

4. You won't be able to (call) (on) or solicit from any of our clients.

5. I'm confident that you'll understand what I'm (getting) (at).

請再聽一次《Track 42》的會話後回答下面問題。

1. Balmert 首先對於合約上的哪一點內容質疑?
   (A) 禁止個人私下利用工作上所學得的知識
   (B) 禁止離職或被解雇的員工搶走公司的客戶
   (C) 禁止離職或被解雇的員工到競爭的同行工作

2. 為什麼 Balmert 對於終止聘雇合約後的補償金問題有所顧慮?
   (A) 因為補償金額太低
   (B) 因為只能得到六個月的遣散費
   (C) 因為被解雇後無法立即獲得

3. Balmert 最後決定怎麼做?
   (A) 要求更改合約內容
   (B) 準備簽約
   (C) 放棄這次工作機會,再找新工作

解答　　　　　　　　　　　　　　　1. (C)　2. (B)　3. (B)

Speaking

會話

 請再聽一次《Track 42》。

Garner: Good morning, Mr. Balmert. I'm glad that we could get together to go over a few documents before you start your new position here at Franklin, Inc.

Balmert: I'm happy to be here. I'm very excited about my new job.

Garner: Good. Well, let's get through this paperwork so that you can get started on your real job as a sales representative here. All of our employees are required to sign a confidentiality, non-solicitation agreement. Are you familiar with those?

Balmert: I've heard of them, but I've never been required to sign one.

Garner: Basically, we believe that our client bases, contact lists and pricing structures are highly proprietary. After training you, we don't believe that you should be able to take that information and use it for your own benefit or use it against the company. That makes sense, doesn't it?

Balmert: Yes, to a certain degree. But, I'm not sure I understand how such an agreement directly affects me.

Garner: Well, it'll govern your behavior in several instances should you ever leave Franklin, Inc. or be laid off. For a period of one year you won't be able to work with any of our competitors. You won't be able to call on or solicit from any of our clients and you'll be legally liable if you spread derogatory information about the company.

Balmert: I understand about the solicitation and the derogatory information, but I'm not quite sure I follow the logic behind the idea of not working for a competitor. If I get laid off, it would be natural for me to go to a similar company since this is my specialty.

Garner: While it may seem natural to you, it would be against our contractual agreement because it requires that you do not work for a competitor for one year after employment termination here. If you think about intellectual property protection and trade secret theft, I'm confident that you'll understand what I'm getting at.

Balmert: Right. My only concern is what happens to me financially if I'm laid off here and can't work in my designated career field for one year?

Garner: Well, that is why we include a generous severance package in the unlikely event that you do get laid off. You'll receive six months of salary as compensation.

Balmert: I understand. What do I do about the remaining six months?

Garner: It's hard to say. Perhaps you'll get recalled. Perhaps you'll make other arrangements yourself. There is no way around this agreement, Mr. Balmert. If you're going to work for us, we must have it signed today.

Balmert: All right. I guess I'll just have to hope that no layoffs are upcoming and that if they are, I can manage the six months out of this field. I'm ready to sign the agreement.

中　譯 ··

嘉　納：包莫特先生，早安。很高興在你到法蘭克林公司正式上
　　　　班前，有這個機會和你見面，一同看一些文件。

包莫特：這是我的榮幸，我非常期待這份新工作。

嘉　納：很好。那我們就一起看這些書面資料，這樣你才可以正
　　　　式開始業務代表的工作。我們所有的員工都必須簽一份

有關保密及禁止拉攏客戶的合約。你清楚這類文件嗎？

包莫特：聽過，但是從來沒有被要求過簽這種合約。

嘉　納：基本上，公司認為我們的基本客戶群、聯絡名單、價格結構都是極為私人的財產。公司不認為經過訓練過後的員工有權利把這些資訊挪為己用、謀求私利，或用來做出對公司不利的舉動。這很合理，不是嗎？

包莫特：某種程度來講是沒錯。不過我還是很不清楚，這樣一份合約會對我有什麼直接影響。

嘉　納：假設你離開法蘭克林公司，或被公司解雇時，這份合約將就幾方面約束你的行為。一年以內你不得為我們公司的競爭同業工作，也不可以拜訪或拉攏我們的客戶，如果四處散播對公司不利的消息，還得負法律責任。

包莫特：拉攏客戶和散播不利消息的部分我能了解，不過我不太懂不准為同行工作背後的道理。因為如果我被解雇，理所當然地我會到同類型的公司工作，畢竟銷售是我的專長。

嘉　納：對你來說這可能是理所當然，但是就違反了我們的合約內容，因為合約要求員工在終止聘雇關係後，一年內不得為競爭對手工作。如果你再想想保護智慧財產和竊取商業機密的事，我想你應該就會了解我的意思。

包莫特：嗯，我唯一顧慮的就是萬一在這裡被解雇了，一年內又無法在自己選定的職場領域工作，那經濟來源怎麼辦？

嘉　納：這就是為什麼我們提供優厚的遣散方案。我們不太可能炒你魷魚，但萬一你真的被解雇，你可以領取六個月薪資作為補償。

包莫特：我了解了。那另外六個月怎麼辦？

嘉　納：這很難說，也許公司會重新雇用你，也許你自己有其他
　　　　安排。包莫特先生，這份合約是必要文件。如果你要為
　　　　我們工作，就一定得在今天簽這份合約。

包莫特：好吧，我想我只能希望未來不會有解雇問題，如果真被
　　　　解雇的話，另外六個月的時間只好再想辦法找其他領域
　　　　的工作。我準備好要簽約了。

語　法 ⋯⋯⋯⋯⋯⋯⋯⋯⋯⋯⋯⋯⋯⋯⋯⋯⋯⋯⋯⋯⋯⋯⋯⋯⋯⋯

● sales representative　（業務代表）
　這個詞彙比 salesman 更正式。重視男女平等的美國，有喜愛用 sales
　representative 甚於 salesman 的傾向。

● should you ever...　（萬一你⋯）
　我們通常會用 if 子句表示假設或條件，其實除了 if 子句表條件外，
　還可以將主詞和（助）動詞倒裝，例如會話中 should you ever leave
　Franklin, Inc. 的句子，其意思是「萬一你離開法蘭克林公司的話」。可
　以利用倒裝表條件的常見動詞及助動詞，分別為 were, had, could,
　should 等，置於主詞之前。例句如：Were I a bird, I could fly to you.
　（如果我是隻小鳥，就能飛到你身邊）/ Should anyone call, tell them
　I'm out to lunch.（萬一有人打電話來，就說我外出用餐了）。

Speaking Function 6

確認是否真正理解的說法

 請聽《Track 45》。

1. A: I'm not sure I understand. Does that mean I can't work for
　　any company in the advertising industry for a year?
　B: Not quite, Mr. Thompson.

2. A: Does this mean I have to live for six months without any pay?

   B: Not exactly.

3. A: Do you see what I mean?

   B: Yes, I think so.

解說

● 要表達出不知自己是否理解對方所講的話，可以說 I'm not sure I understand. Does that mean...?。Does that mean 的部分可以因應不同情況改換成 Does this mean 或 Do you mean，或者可如本章會話中 I'm not sure I understand how such an agreement directly affects me. 的句子，在 understand 之後接續以疑問詞引導的子句。

● Does that/this mean...? 和 Do you mean...? 可以改換成 So what you mean is... Right?（所以你的意思是…對吧?）。又「換句話說是…吧?」的英語是 In other words... Right?；而「…我這樣說沒錯吧?」則是 So am I right in saying...? / Would I be correct in saying...?。

● 想確認對方是否了解自己所說的內容，可用 Do you see what I mean? / Do you know what I mean?，以及 Do you understand what I mean? 的表達方式。動詞 mean 的部分也可替換成片語 drive at，即說成 Do you know what I'm driving at?。另外在會話中可經常聽到 Am I making myself clear?；若要用其他片語表達，還可說成 Does that seem to make sense?。

練習 1【代換】

 請隨《Track 46》做代換練習。

  1. I'm not sure I understand.

    Does that mean I have to buy more than ten of these?

    Does that mean I must pay for it in advance?

Does that mean I need to get permission to use this room?
Does that mean I can't fly business class?

2. *Does this mean* I have to live for six months without any pay from the company?
Do you mean...?
So what you mean is... Right?
In other words, ... Right?
So am I right in saying...?

3. *"Do you see what I mean?"*   "Yes, I do."
"Do you know what I mean?"
"Do you understand what I mean?"
"Do you know what I'm driving at?"

練習 2【角色扮演】

 請隨《Track 47》在嗶一聲後唸出灰色部分的句子。

1. A: I'm not sure I understand. Does that mean I can't speak to any of your customers if I'm laid off?

   B: That's right, Mr. Thompson.

2. A: Does this mean while I'm in the office I can't visit websites for my personal use?

   B: I'm afraid so.

3. A: Do you see what I mean?

   B: No, I'm afraid I don't.

練習 3【覆誦重要語句】

請隨《Track 48》覆誦英文句子。

1. go over 「察看」
   ↳Let's go over the agreement to make sure there won't be any misunderstandings between us.
   （我們一起來看這份合約，確定雙方沒有任何誤解。）

2. get through 「完成」
   ↳Let's get through this paperwork as quickly as possible because we have a lot of important things to do.（我們趕快把這份書面作業處理完，因為還有許多重要的事要做。）

3. get started 「開始」
   ↳I think you should get started on that market analysis right away.（我想你應該馬上開始進行那份市場分析。）

4. be familiar with 「熟悉」
   ↳I wonder if you are familiar with the American tax system.（我不知道你對美國稅制熟不熟。）

5. for ～'s benefit 「為了～的利益著想」
   ↳One half of the money collected by the charity group was spent for the benefit of the homeless in town.
   （這個慈善團體有一半的募款是用在鎮上的遊民身上。）

6. to a certain degree 「某種程度上」
   ↳I understand your argument to a certain degree, but I think you should give in to them this time.（某種程度上，我能了解你的論點，不過我覺得這次你應該對他們讓步。）

7. call on 「拜訪」

↳ Why don't you call on my cousin when you are in Hawaii? (你到夏威夷的時候，何不去找我表姐?)

8. get laid off 「被解雇」

↳ He suddenly got laid off after years of faithful service to his company.

(多年來他一直對公司忠心耿耿，沒想到卻突然遭解雇。)

9. seem natural 「似乎是理所當然的」

↳ It seems natural to you, but putting yourself first is taken as a disharmonious act in our culture. (這對你來說似乎是理所當然，但是在我們的文化裡，老把自己擺第一位是種不合群的行為。)

10. get at 「意指」

↳ What are you getting at when you say we have to prepare for the upcoming recession? (你說我們要準備好面對即將來臨的經濟衰退，指的是什麼?)

實力測驗

有一天，你的經理召集了所有部門同仁宣布一項加班的新規定，內容如下：今後仍按照原有的規定，每個星期至少必須加班 3 個鐘頭，但加班津貼則是超過 10 個鐘頭者才能發給。對於這項規定，你有些不太明白，請用三種不同的說法詢問經理的意見。

1. I'm not sure I understand. Does that mean we work for five hours for nothing every week?

2. So what you mean is we work for five hours for nothing every week. Right?

3. In other words, we work for five hours for nothing every week. Right?

Chapter 7

Buying a House 買房子

Listening

Warm-up / Pre-questions

 請聽《Track 49》的廣告後回答下面問題。

為什麼現在買房子很划得來?
- (A) 因為房子價格便宜
- (B) 因為房貸利率下跌
- (C) 因為已經開放每個人可以向銀行長期貸款

內容　Mortgage rates have fallen by 1.2 percent over the past twelve months. That means that you can save $150 each month on a $150,000 home loan.

Add to this the fact that average home values went up six percent last year. Increased values and tax benefits combine to make owning a house a great opportunity for an enhanced lifestyle. Call me soon at 206–894–9000 to discover how simple it can be to purchase a home right now. Today's great mortgage rates make buying a home easier than ever.

中譯　過去十二個月以來,抵押貸款的利率下降了 1.2%,這表示 15 萬美元的房貸每月可省下 150 美元。
再加上去年房屋平均價格升值 6%,房屋價格增值,又加上稅賦優惠,這麼一來擁有房子就成為提升生活品質的一大良機。請儘快電洽 206–894–9000,馬上為您說明現在購屋有多容易。目前低廉的抵押貸款利率讓購屋比以前來得更輕鬆。

Listening Step 1

 請聽《Track 50》的會話後回答下面問題。

Doug 和 Cindy 正有什麼打算？

(A) 賣掉舊屋，換購新屋

(B) 買別墅居住

(C) 不再租房子，要買屬於自己的房子

解答 (C)

Listening Step 2

熟悉下列關鍵字

rent　租賃
real estate agent　房地產公司
mortgage company　抵押貸款公司
pre-qualify　事先審核資格
price range　價格範圍
tax benefit　稅賦優惠
tax deduction　稅賦減免，扣除額
detail　細節

saving 節省
pay stub 薪資單
accurate 正確的
debt 負債
process 手續，程序

1 請聽《Track 51》並在括弧內填入正確答案。

1. Was the advertisement from a (　　　) (　　　) agent?
2. Actually, it was from a (　　　) company.
3. I know that you get a big tax (　　　) from owning a home.
4. I'm just not sure about the (　　　) of the savings.
5. They'll probably want to know about the (　　　) that we owe as well.

解答

1. Was the advertisement from a (real) (estate) agent?
2. Actually, it was from a (mortgage) company.
3. I know that you get a big tax (deduction) from owning a home.
4. I'm just not sure about the (details) of the savings.
5. They'll probably want to know about the (debt) that we owe as well.

1 請再聽一次《Track 50》的會話後回答下面問題。

1. 房貸利率下降了多少？
   (A) 1.2%
   (B) 3%
   (C) 6%

2. Cindy 看到的廣告是什麼廣告?

    (A) 房屋仲介業者的廣告

    (B) 抵押貸款公司的廣告

    (C) 土地開發業者的廣告

解答   1. (A)   2. (B)

Listening Step 3

熟悉下列語句

have got to   必須

of one's own   自己的

take some action   採取一些行動

be all right with   ～是可以的

be fine by   ～是沒關係的

hear of   聽說

1 請聽《Track 52》並在括弧內填入正確答案。

    1. We've got to stop renting and buy a place (   ) (   ) (   ).

    2. We really need to (   ) (   ) (   ) right away.

    3. Is it (   ) (   ) (   ) you if I call?

    4. It's (   ) (   ) me.

    5. I've never (   ) (   ) them before.

解答

1. We've got to stop renting and buy a place (of) (our) (own).

2. We really need to (take) (some) (action) right away.

3. Is it (all) (right) (with) you if I call?

4. It's (fine) (by) me.

5. I've never (heard) (of) them before.

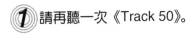請再聽一次《Track 50》的會話後回答下面問題。

1. 為什麼 Doug 說要趁現在買房子?

   (A) 有很多舊房子在出售,機會難得

   (B) 房子價格在上漲,而房貸利率降低

   (C) 房價急速暴漲,現在再不買會後悔一輩子

2. 購買房子會有什麼好處?

   (A) 有稅賦上的優惠

   (B) 增加住宅津貼

   (C) 享有更多的居住自由

3. Cindy 打算隔天做什麼?

   (A) 去看待售房屋

   (B) 請銀行開存款餘額證明

   (C) 打電話給抵押貸款公司

解答   1. (B)   2. (A)   3. (C)

Speaking

會話

請再聽一次《Track 50》。

Doug: Cindy, we've got to stop renting and buy a place of our own. Don't you think so?

Cindy: That's just what I was thinking. I saw an advertisement in the paper today that said house prices have increased 6 percent this year while mortgage rates have dropped 1.2 percent.

Doug: That's unbelievable. We really need to take some action right away. Was the advertisement from a real estate agent?

Cindy: No. Actually, it was from a mortgage company.

Doug: I guess the mortgage company pre-qualifies you for a loan and then you know the price range to begin looking at.

Cindy: That makes sense. I still have the advertisement in the car. I really think we should call tomorrow and get this started. Is it all right with you if I call?

Doug: It's fine by me. What's the name of the mortgage company?

Cindy: Something like, "Homes and Neighbors Mortgage."

Doug: I've never heard of them before. When you call, could you ask about the tax benefits as well?

Cindy: That's a great idea. I know that you get a big tax deduction from owning a home. I'm just not sure about the details of the savings.

Doug: You'll probably need our pay stubs when you call so you can give them accurate information about how much money we make.

Cindy: That's true. They'll probably want to know about the debt that we owe as well—cars, credit cards, and student loans.

Doug: I'm sure they will. Let's get everything together now so you can call tomorrow. I really want to get this house buying process started.

Cindy: So do I. I can't wait to stop renting and get into our own home.

中　譯

道格：辛蒂，我們不該再租房子了，應該買自己的房子，妳覺得呢？

辛蒂：我正好也在想這件事。今天我在報紙上看到一則廣告說，今年房價上漲6%，而抵押貸款利率降了1.2%。

道格：真不敢相信，我們動作得快了。那則廣告是房地產公司登的嗎？

辛蒂：不是，是一家抵押貸款公司。

道格：我想貸款公司一定會事先查核貸款人資格，提供我們房價的範圍，我們就可以開始找房子了。

辛蒂：有道理。那則廣告還在車裡。我真的覺得我們明天就該打電話去問，早點開始。我來打電話，你覺得怎樣？

道格：可以啊。那家抵押貸款公司的名字是什麼？

辛蒂：好像是「房屋鄰居抵押貸款公司」。

道格：沒聽過。你打電話過去的時候，可不可以順便問問有沒有稅賦優惠？

辛蒂：好主意，我知道擁有房子可以減免不少稅，只是不曉得實際上能省多少錢。

道格：打電話的時候，妳可能需要用到我們的薪資單，這樣妳才能跟他們說明我們的確切收入有多少。

辛蒂：那倒是，而且說不定他們還想知道我們的負債情形──像

　　　　汽車貸款、信用卡額度、助學貸款。

道格： 我肯定他們一定會問。我們先把資料整理好，妳明天就可
　　　 以打電話了。真想趕快進行買房子的手續。

辛蒂： 我也是。我等不及要搬進我們自己的窩，不用再租房子了。

語　法

- have got to　（必須）

  have got to 是 have to 的非正式口語的說法，但注意不可與助動詞連
  用。也就是可以說 You might have to go there.（你可能必須跑一趟），
  但切記不可說成 You might have got to go there.。

- stop renting　（不再租房子）

  stop + V.ing 是「停止做某事」的意思，如 He stopped smoking.（他不
  抽菸了）；stop to do 則是指「停下來去做某事」，如 He stopped to
  smoke.（他停下來，抽起了菸）。要留意雖然可以說 It stopped raining.
  （雨停了），但不可說成 It stopped to rain.。

Speaking Function 7

表示同意或不同意的說法

請聽《Track 53》。

1. A: We've got to buy a house right away. Don't you think so?

   B: That's just what I was thinking.

2. A: I think this house is too expensive for us.

   B: Yes, I agree.

3. A: We want a house with a swimming pool in the yard. Don't
   you agree?

   B: No, I don't agree.

解說

● 要徵求對方的同意時，通常可以採用附加問句的形式，例如：This is too expensive, isn't it?。其實也有別於此種表達方式，例如敘述完自我的意見之後，說句 Don't you agree?。除此之外，也可以使用 Don't you feel so? / Wouldn't you say so? / Don't you go along with that? / Right? 等說法。

● 表示同意的基本慣用句除了 Yes, I agree. 之外，還有 That's right. 和 That's quite right. 等。簡單省略的說法則有 True enough. / How true. / Oh. Exactly. 等等。而 I'm with you there. / I'm of exactly the same opinion. / I can't help thinking the same thing. 等句子，可以說是維持良好人際關係的精鍊措辭。

● 表示不同意的基本句是 No, I don't agree.，另外 No, I don't think so. 也經常被使用。Not really. 和 I'm not sure, actually. 等是表示輕微的不同意；(I'm afraid,) I disagree. 則是表示強烈的不同意。

練習 1【代換】

 請隨《Track 54》做代換練習。

1. About buying a house, we'd better wait for another year.
   Don't you think so?
   Don't you agree?
   Don't you feel so?
   Wouldn't you say so?
   Do you go along with that?

2. "I think the kitchen should be redone before we move in."
   "Yes, I agree."
   "That's quite right."

"True enough."
"How true."
"Oh. Exactly."
"I'm with you there."
"I'm of exactly the same opinion."

3. "We should sell this house and buy a condo downtown. Don't you agree?"

"No, I don't agree."

"Not really."
"I'm not sure, actually."
"No, I don't think so."
"I'm afraid, I disagree."
"I don't think that's a good idea."

練習 2 【角色扮演】

請隨《Track 55》在嗶一聲後唸出灰色部分的句子。

1. A: We've got to buy a holiday cottage in the country. Don't you think so?

   B: That's just what I was thinking.

2. A: I think we should look for a less expensive house.

   B: Yes, I agree.

3. A: A house seems better than a condo. Don't you agree?

   B: I don't agree.

練習 3【覆誦重要語句】

 請隨《Track 56》覆誦英文句子。

1. have got to 「必須」
   ↳We've got to refurbish the house if we want to sell it at a good price.（如果想要讓這房子賣個好價錢，我們就得重新整修一番。）

2. rent 「租賃」
   ↳I prefer renting an apartment in an urban area to buying a house in the suburbs.
   （我寧可在市區租房子，也不想在郊區買房子。）

3. of one's own 「自己的」
   ↳Jack wants to have a car of his own so that he can drive anywhere, anytime he wants.（傑克想擁有自己的車子，這樣他就可以隨時到任何想去的地方。）

4. take some action 「採取某些行動」
   ↳We should take some action before things get worse.
   （在情況惡化之前，我們應該採取某些行動。）

5. price range 「價格範圍」
   ↳I'd like to know the price range of a four-bedroom house.
   （我想知道有四個房間的房屋價位如何。）

6. be all right with 「～是可以的」
   ↳Is it all right with you if I try to get the house loan at our bank?（如果我向我們的銀行申請房貸，你覺得好嗎?）

7. hear of 「聽說」
   ↳I've never heard of buying a house without a down payment.（我從來沒聽說過買房子不需要頭期款。）

8. detail 「細節」

↳ I'm really interested in buying a house so will you send me all the details?

（我很有意願買間房子，你可不可以寄詳細資料給我?）

9. debt 「負債」

↳ The average consumer is holding about $3,500 in debt on five or six credit cards.（平均而言，每位消費者約有五、六張信用卡，背負著 3500 美元的債務。）

10. get ～ together 「整理」

↳ Will you get all the necessary documents for the meeting together while I talk to my client?（在我和客戶面談時，你可不可以準備好這次會議要用的所有必要文件?）

實力測驗

你的朋友建議你可以趁現在房市低迷、房子最便宜的時候買間房子，但你抱持相反的意見，認為房價在二、三年內還會持續滑落。請用三種不同的說法來表示你的不同意。

參考解答　1. I'm afraid, I don't agree. I think house prices will continue to drop for another two or three years.
2. No, I don't think so.
3. I don't think that's right.

Chapter 8

Retirement Plan 退休計畫

Listening

Warm-up / Pre-questions

請聽《Track 57》的廣告後回答下面問題。

這段廣告鎖定的對象是哪些人?
- (A) 有貸款煩惱的人
- (B) 考慮自行創業的人
- (C) 思考未來理財計畫的人

內容　Remember when you used to tell yourself that if you had money you wouldn't have any troubles? Well, the reality is that money is a pretty complicated thing. Now that you have some money, you have built up a certain amount of net worth, you may be asking yourself different questions. You may be wondering, "Is my money working hard enough for me"? "How can I use the money I have accumulated to free up more of my time?" "What financial strategies can I begin on my own and where do I need help?"

At Astro Financial we have the answers to those questions and many more. No matter what your financial issue—a retirement to plan, options to exercise, or capital gains to manage—your Astro Financial advisor can help you make a plan that benefits every aspect of your financial life. Contact Astro Financial today and let us help you increase your time and your money.

中譯　您是否曾告訴自己，一旦有錢就沒煩惱了？然而事實上，金錢
　　　是種複雜難懂的東西。既然現在有了錢，已經累積了一定數量
　　　的財富，問題可能不同了。您或許會思考：「我的財富價值是否
　　　已充分運用？」或「我該如何利用累積的財富節省更多的時間？」
　　　「有什麼理財方法可以讓我自己著手規劃實行？我又會在哪些
　　　部分需要協助？」
　　　讓艾斯多理財投資顧問公司為您解答這方面的疑惑。不管您的
　　　問題是什麼——舉凡退休計畫、選擇權買賣、資本利得管理等
　　　等。艾斯多理財投資專業顧問將協助您打造周全計畫，讓您的
　　　理財面面俱到。現在就聯絡艾斯多，讓我們幫您贏得更多的時
　　　間和金錢。

解答　(C)

解說　"if you had money you wouldn't have any troubles" 是假設法過
　　　去式的句子，假設對方曾經這麼認為："If I had money, I
　　　wouldn't have any troubles."。所謂假設法過去式是與現在事實
　　　相反的假設，表示「如果～就…」之意。"No matter what your
　　　financial issue..."（不管你的理財問題是什麼）這句話中的 issue
　　　之後，亦可加上 is。而 options to exercise 的 option 是指 stock
　　　option（股票選擇權）。其他字義：used to「過去常做」、reality
　　　「事實」、complicated「複雜的」、now that「既然」、build up「建
　　　立」、net worth「淨資產」、accumulate「儲存」、free up「解放」、
　　　strategy「策略」、on my own「自行」、No matter what「不管」、
　　　retirement「退休」、exercise「行使」、capital gain「資本利得」，
　　　而 aspect 為「方面」之意。

Listening Step 1

1 請聽《Track 58》的會話後回答下面問題。

Hobson 女士正在詢問什麼事?
  (A) 如何提升自己的學經歷
  (B) 如何擬定退休理財計畫
  (C) 如何轉換房貸合約

解答   (B)

Listening Step 2

熟悉下列關鍵字

financial advisor　理財顧問
retire　退休
maintain　維持
current　目前的
fear　害怕，恐懼
share　共有
globe　全球
retirement　退休
social security　社會福利
homemaker　家庭主婦
temporary　臨時的
retirement benefits　退休福利金
tough situation　困難的狀況
asset　資產
condominium　各戶有獨立產權的公寓；分戶租售的公寓
worth　有～價值的
owe　欠（債等）；對～負有償還的義務
equity　資產淨值
terrified　害怕的

financial plan　理財計畫
investment　投資
relieved　放心的

① 請聽《Track 59》並在括弧內填入正確答案。

1. I'm afraid that when it's time for me to (　　　) I won't be able to maintain my current standard of living.
2. I was a (　　　) up until 7 years ago.
3. I have a 1-bedroom condominium that is (　　　) $115,000 and I owe $55,000 on it.
4. So you have about $60,000 in (　　), correct?
5. And that's why I'm (　　) of retirement.

解答
1. I'm afraid that when it's time for me to (retire) I won't be able to maintain my current standard of living.
2. I was a (homemaker) up until 7 years ago.
3. I have a 1-bedroom condominium that is (worth) $115,000 and I owe $55,000 on it.
4. So you have about $60,000 in (equity), correct?
5. And that's why I'm (terrified) of retirement.

① 請再聽一次《Track 58》的會話後回答下面問題。

1. Hobson 女士的職業是什麼?
  (A) 家庭主婦
  (B) 教師
  (C) 公寓管理員

2. Hobson 女士有多少淨資產?

   (A) $55,000

   (B) $60,000

   (C) $115,000

解答   1. (B)   2. (B)

Listening Step 3

熟悉下列語句

what brings you to...   為什麼來…

to speak of   （用於否定句）值得一提的

because of   因為

at all   （用於疑問句）究竟；（用於否定句）一點也

come up with   提出

put together   彙整

1 請聽《Track 60》並在括弧內填入正確答案。

1. Good afternoon, Ms. Hobson and (   ) (   ) (   ) to Astro Financial today?

2. I don't really have any retirement to (   ) (   ) besides social security.

3. You're in a tough situation. Do you have any assets (   ) (   )?

4. It sounds like we need to (   ) (   ) (   ) a personal financial plan for you.

5. We can certainly (   ) (   ) (   ) (   ) for

you that will have you retiring comfortably in the next 15 years.

1 請再聽一次《Track 58》的會話後回答下面問題。

1. Hobson 女士為什麼會在七年前開始教書?
   (A) 因為丈夫過世,失去經濟的依靠
   (B) 因為不需再照顧小孩
   (C) 因為想到老後的日子,覺得還是有份工作比較好

2. Hobson 女士之所以無法擔任專任教師的理由可能是什麼?
   (A) 資格不夠
   (B) 49 歲的她,年紀偏大
   (C) 太過專心管理自己的公寓

3. 理財顧問認為 Hobson 女士的經濟狀況如何?
   (A) 經濟狀況良好
   (B) 經濟狀況不佳
   (C) 理財能力欠佳

解答   1. (A)   2. (B)   3. (B)

Speaking

會話

 請再聽一次《Track 58》。

Financial Advisor: Good afternoon, Ms. Hobson and what brings you to Astro Financial today?

Ms. Hobson: I'm afraid that when it's time for me to retire I won't be able to maintain my current standard of living.

Financial Advisor: Well, that's certainly a fear shared by many people around the globe! Tell me about your financial situation so far.

Ms. Hobson: All right. I'm 49 years old and I don't really have any retirement to speak of besides social security. That is not much because I was a homemaker up until 7 years ago when my husband died and I went back to work.

Financial Advisor: I see. And what kind of work do you do?

Ms. Hobson: I'm a high school teacher, but I've only been able to get temporary part-time positions—perhaps because of my age —and they don't offer any retirement benefits. On a part-time teacher's salary I haven't been able to save any money for retirement, either.

Financial Advisor: You're in a tough situation. Do you have any assets at all?

Ms. Hobson: Yes, I have a 1-bedroom condominium that is worth $115,000 and I owe $55,000 on it.

Financial Advisor: So you have $60,000 in equity, correct?

Ms. Hobson: Yes. And that's why I'm terrified of retirement. I am not prepared.

Financial Advisor: It sounds like we need to come up with a personal financial plan for you that includes retirement planning and specific investment strategies.

Ms. Hobson: That's exactly what I need. Can you help me?

Financial Advisor: Don't worry, Ms. Hobson. You've come to the right place. We can certainly put a plan together for you that will have you retiring comfortably in the next 15 years. You have a late start, but we can come up with something that will work for you.

Ms. Hobson: Thank you. I'm so relieved. What do I need to do next?

中　譯

理財顧問：午安，哈布森女士。請問您今天到艾斯多理財顧問公司來有什麼事？

哈布森：我怕到我退休的時候，沒辦法維持現在的生活水準。

理財顧問：的確，這種恐懼世界各地人人都有。請先描述一下您目前的財務狀況。

哈布森：好的。我現在49歲，除了社會福利外，談不上有其他的退休金。這是因為我原先是家庭主婦，一直到七年前我先生過世，才又出來工作。

理財顧問：原來如此，那您從事什麼樣的工作？

哈布森：我是中學老師，可能是年紀的關係，只能得到臨時兼

職的工作，並且學校不提供任何退休金。單靠兼職教
師的薪水，也存不了什麼錢留作退休用。

理財顧問：您的處境確實困難。有沒有任何資產？

哈 布 森：有，我有一間單房小公寓，價值 11 萬 5 千美元，不過
還要繳 5 萬 5 千元貸款。

理財顧問：所以您擁有 6 萬元淨資產，對吧？

哈 布 森：是的，這就是為什麼我一想到退休就害怕。我還沒有
準備好。

理財顧問：這樣聽起來，有必要幫您設計一套個人理財方案，包
括退休計畫和特定投資計畫。

哈 布 森：那正是我所需要的。您能幫助我嗎？

理財顧問：別擔心，哈布森女士。您來對地方了。我們當然能幫
您擬定計畫，讓您 15 年後可以安心退休，無後顧之憂。
雖然開始得晚，不過我們可以一起想辦法，找出合適
的計畫。

哈 布 森：謝謝，我終於放心了。接下來我需要做什麼？

語　法

● What brings you to Astro Financial today? （請問您今天到艾斯多理財
顧問公司來有什麼事？）

店員以及公司職員對於顧客的第一句問候語通常是 May I help you?。
若要問明有什麼要事時，可以 what 為主詞，說 What brings you to ～
today? 的句子。留意動詞需用現在式，不可用過去式。此外，最好不
要使用 Why did you com here today? 等含有盤問語氣的句子，以免無
禮。

● any retirement to speak of （沒有任何退休金可言）

從整段會話的上下文來看，retirement 是指 retirement benefits 而言。

- a plan...that will have you retiring comfortably in the next 15 years. （這個計畫讓您 15 年後可以安心退休。）

此句話的 have 是使役動詞。使役動詞的補語通常使用省略 to 的不定詞，但有時也可接續現在分詞，例如：He *had* me do all sorts of work for him. [不帶 to 的不定詞] / He *had* me doing all sorts of work for him. [現在分詞] （他要我幫他做各種工作）。

Speaking Function 8

表示擔心與害怕的說法

請聽《Track 61》。

1. A: What's the matter?

   B: I'm worried about the project.

2. A: I'm worried that I may not meet the deadline on this report.

   B: I'm sure you can make it.

3. A: I'm terrified of losing my present job.

   B: Don't worry. You'll never lose it.

解說
- 敘述擔心某件事的基本慣用句是 I'm worried about ～, worried 一字可替換成 uneasy, concerned, anxious, apprehensive 等。uneasy 是表「心神不寧, 靜不下來」、concerned 是「對事情感到憂心忡忡」, 而 anxious 帶有「對還未發生的事杞人憂天」的意味, apprehensive 則是比較正式的用語。
- 「擔心是否…」的英語說法, 是在 worried 之後連接從屬子句, 而連接詞 that 經常會被省略, 如 I'm worried (that) I may not meet the deadline on this report. （我擔心無法趕上交報告的期限）即是

一例。
● 「害怕～」的基本句型是 I'm afraid of ～，afraid 可以改換成 terrified, frightened, scared, nervous, fearful 等字。表單純害怕的 afraid 是一般最常見到的字，scared 則是僅次於其後的常用字；terrified 是表「非常害怕的」、frightened 是表「短暫的害怕」，而 nervous 是表「緊張不安的狀態」，fearful 則是比較正式的用語。

練習 1【代換】

 請隨《Track 62》做代換練習。

1. *I'm worried about*　　my retirement plan.
　I'm uneasy about
　I'm concerned about
　I'm anxious about
　I'm apprehensive about

2. *I'm worried*　　that I won't be able to maintain my current standard of living.
　I'm uneasy
　I'm concerned
　I'm anxious

3. *I'm terrified of*　　retirement because I'm not prepared.
　I'm frightened of
　I'm afraid of
　I'm scared of

練習2【角色扮演】

① 請隨《Track 63》在嗶一聲後唸出灰色部分的句子。

1. A: What's the matter?

   B: I'm worried about the health of my aging mother.

2. A: I'm worried that I may be late for my plane.

   B: Don't worry. There's a lot of time.

3. A: I'm terrified of flying.

   B: Are you kidding? Planes are very safe.

練習3【覆誦重要語句】

① 請隨《Track 64》覆誦英文句子。

1. retire 「退休」

   ↳Mr. Johnson retired at the age of 65 and is now working part-time at the museum.

   （強森先生65歲退休，目前在博物館兼差。）

2. maintain 「維持」

   ↳He maintained close contact with his family and friends living at a distance.

   （他和住在遠方的家人及朋友保持密切聯繫。）

3. to speak of 「（用於否定句）值得一提的」

   ↳I'm afraid I have no ability to speak of.

   （我恐怕自己沒有什麼值得一提的才能。）

4. because of 「因為」

   ↳My flight from San Francisco to New York was canceled because of a dense fog. （因為濃霧的關係，我原本要搭從

舊金山飛往紐約的班機取消了。)

5. be in a tough situation 「處境困難」
  ↳Financially he was in a tough situation, but he tried to remain optimistic.
  (即使財務狀況困難，他仍盡量保持樂觀。)

6. at all 「(用於疑問句)究竟」
  ↳Does he have any interest in business at all?
  (他究竟對生意有沒有興趣?)

7. worth 「有～價值的」
  ↳The property was only worth about $200,000 at the time, but now it's worth $600,000. (當時這塊房地產只價值約 20 萬美元，現在已經飆漲到 60 萬美元了。)

8. come up with 「提出」
  ↳He came up with a very impressive solution to the manpower shortage problem.
  (他提出了非常好的辦法來解決人手不足的問題。)

9. put together 「彙整」
  ↳We have to put together a proposal to streamline the management.
  (我們必須彙整出一套能有效提昇管理效能的提案。)

10. relieved 「放心的」
  ↳Mr. Holmes was relieved to hear that he didn't have to go into hospital.
  (荷姆斯先生聽到自己不用住院後，大大地鬆了一口氣。)

實力測驗

你很擔心萬一自職場退休後，沒有足夠的錢過寬裕自在的老年生活，你一直為此感到心情鬱悶。這時一位同事注意到你無精打采的神情，很關心地問你 What's the matter with you?，請用三種不同的說法回應他的關心。

參考解答
1. I'm worried that I won't have enough money to live in comfort after my retirement.
2. I'm uneasy that I won't have enough money to live in comfort after my retirement.
3. I'm concerned that I won't have enough money to live in comfort after my retirement.

Chapter 9

Alternative Medicine　另類醫療

Listening

Warm-up / Pre-questions

 請聽《Track 1》的廣告後回答下面問題。

這段廣告主要針對的對象是哪些人?

(A) 為病煩惱的人

(B) 西醫主張已無康復可能的病患

(C) 對中醫草藥有興趣的醫生們

內容　Herbs are the natural way to strengthen, nourish, and balance the body. They give your body the vital life force that helps it heal itself. Herbs don't have any harmful side effects when taken correctly. When you combine herbs with good nutrition, you improve your health and well-being.

Healing Herbs has just opened a new store on Jamison St. and 1st Ave. We invite you to stop in and discover what herbs can do for you. We carry single herbs, herbal combinations, Chinese formulas and a full line of additional products—books, essential oils and homeopathic remedies. We also have an on-site acupuncturist and massage therapist.

中譯　藥草能自然地強化、滋補、平衡身體,使您活力充沛,抵抗力強。只要正確服用,絕不會產生任何有害的副作用。藥草再搭配充足的營養攝取,能讓您更健康更舒暢。

「草本百匯」新店開幕,位於傑米森街和第一大道的交叉路口

上。我們誠摯邀請您蒞臨參觀，親自體驗藥草的功效。有單種藥草、複方藥草、漢藥配方，還有一系列相關商品——書籍、香精油、順勢療法藥方，現場還有針灸師和按摩師為您服務。

解答　(A)

解說　alternative medicine（另類醫療）是指有別於西醫療法的其他醫療方式，諸如自然食療法、藥草療法及針灸療法等等。well-being 是「健康、幸福」的意思，常與 health 連用，即 health and well-being。要指出一家店或公司的位置是在兩條交叉的路口或其附近時，可如 on Jamison St. and 1st Ave. 使用 on 表示，完整例句如：The restaurant is on Broadway and 14th Street.（這家餐廳位於百老匯和第 14 街的交叉路口上）。single herbs 是指「單種（單一的）藥草」，herbal combinations 則指「（多種藥草成分組合的）複方藥草」；而將能引起類似症狀的藥物少量施打在患者身上進行治療的方法，叫做 homeopathy（順勢療法），homeopathic remedies 則是「順勢療法的藥劑」。其他字義：strengthen「強化」、nourish「滋養」、vital「充滿活力的」、life force「生命力」、heal「治療」、harmful「有害的」、side effect「副作用」、nutrition「營養」、Chinese formula「漢藥配方」、essential oil「香精油」、homeopathic remedy「順勢療法」、on-site「在現場的」、acupuncturist「針灸師」，而 massage therapist 為「按摩師」之意。

Listening Step 1

 請聽《Track 2》的會話後回答下面問題。

Emily 最近的健康狀態如何？
　(A) 很容易生病

(B) 有病，但自己沒有察覺到症狀

(C) 生重病，必須立刻住院

解答 (A)

Listening Step 2

熟悉下列關鍵字

demand　要求
senior accountant　資深會計師
tax time　報稅期間
antibiotics　抗生素
herbal remedy　草本藥方；藥草療法
migraine headache　偏頭痛
recover　復原
feverfew　小白菊
tablet　藥片，藥錠
dissipate　消失
echinacea　紫錐花（多年生菊科草本植物）
immune system　免疫系統

2 請聽《Track 3》並在括弧內填入正確答案。

1. I know the heavy (　　　　) placed on senior accountants during tax time.

2. Taking (　　　　) constantly is not good for your body.

3. I wish I knew more about herbal (　　　　) or some sort of alternative medicine.

4. Do you remember those bad migraine (　　　　) that I used

to have?

5. If I feel a migraine coming on, I take three of the herbal tablets twice a day and the migraine (   ).

解答

1. I know the heavy (demands) placed on senior accountants during tax time.

2. Taking (antibiotics) constantly is not good for your body.

3. I wish I knew more about herbal (remedies) or some sort of alternative medicine.

4. Do you remember those bad migraine (headaches) that I used to have?

5. If I feel a migraine coming on, I take three of the herbal tablets twice a day and the migraine (dissipates).

② 請再聽一次《Track 2》的會話後回答下面問題。

1. Emily 從事什麼工作？
   (A) 推銷
   (B) 市場調查
   (C) 會計

2. Emily 目前正服用什麼藥？
   (A) 抗生素
   (B) 抗癌劑
   (C) 腸胃藥

解答   1. (C)   2. (A)

Listening Step 3

熟悉下列語句

```
under the weather    身體不舒服
be on the medicine   服用藥物
run out    用完
some sort of    某些種類的
at this point    在這個時候，目前
be out of work    停止工作
come on    （疾病等）發作，產生
help out    幫助
```

② 請聽《Track 4》並在括弧內填入正確答案。

1. You look a little bit (　　　) (　　　) (　　　　).

2. I was okay while I was (　　　) (　　　) (　　　), but when it runs out, I just get sick again.

3. I'm willing to try anything (　　　) (　　　) (　　　).

4. You would be (　　　) (　　　) (　　　) for at least two days recovering!

5. I wonder if there is an herb that would (　　　) (　　　) (　　　).

解答

1. You look a little bit (under) (the) (weather).

2. I was okay while I was (on) (the) (medicine), but when it runs out, I just get sick again.

3. I'm willing to try anything (at) (this) (point).

4. You would be (out) (of) (work) for at least two days recovering!

5. I wonder if there is an herb that would (help) (me) (out).

請再聽一次《Track 2》的會話後回答下面問題。

1. 為什麼 Emily 對目前服用的藥有所抱怨？
   (A) 因為吃了也沒效果
   (B) 因為有強烈的副作用
   (C) 因為若沒繼續服用，病就會又復發
2. 為什麼 Rachael 大力推薦藥草？
   (A) 因為她的偏頭痛是藥草治好的
   (B) 因為她男朋友的偏頭痛是藥草治好的
   (C) 因為她常去看病的醫生是有名的中醫師
3. 為什麼 Emily 想知道 Rachael 的男朋友是在哪裡買到藥草的？
   (A) 她想多知道另類療法的事
   (B) 她想了解那家藥店是否值得信賴
   (C) 她想到那家店看看是否有適合自己的藥

解答　　　　　　　　　　　　　　1. (C)　2. (A)　3. (C)

Speaking

會話

 請再聽一次《Track 2》。

Rachael: Hi, Emily. I haven't seen you in weeks. How's it going?
Emily: Hi, Rachael. I'm doing all right, I guess.
Rachael: You look a little bit under the weather. Are you feeling okay?

Emily: No, not really. I've been sick a lot lately. Working such long hours under such pressure isn't helping.

Rachael: Yes, I know the heavy demands placed on senior accountants during tax time. Have you been to see a doctor?

Emily: Yes. I've been in three times and each time the doctor gave me antibiotics. I was okay while I was on the medicine, but when it runs out, I just get sick again.

Rachael: That's too bad. Taking antibiotics constantly is not good for your body either.

Emily: That's what I've read. I wish I knew more about herbal remedies or some sort of alternative medicine. I'm willing to try anything at this point.

Rachael: I don't know too much about alternative medicine either, but do you remember those bad migraine headaches that I used to have?

Emily: Yes, I sure do! You would be out of work for at least two days recovering!

Rachael: Well, my boyfriend got me this herb called feverfew. I don't know where he got it, but if I feel a migraine coming on, I take three of the herbal tablets twice a day and the migraine dissipates. It's amazing.

Emily: I wonder if there is an herb that would help me out.

Rachael: I'm sure there is. Have you ever heard of echinacea? I think that herb builds up the immune system and acts as a natural antibiotic.

Emily: I've heard of that. Can you ask your boyfriend where he got your migraine herb so I can go see what they have to help me?

Rachael: Sure. I'll call Jason right now.

中　譯 ....

瑞　秋：嗨，艾蜜莉。好幾個禮拜沒看到妳了，最近過得怎樣？

艾蜜莉：嗨，瑞秋。還不錯吧，我想。

瑞　秋：可是妳看起來不太舒服耶，還好吧？

艾蜜莉：嗯，其實不太好，最近經常生病。在有壓力的情況下工作得很晚，病是好不了的。

瑞　秋：我知道報稅期間，資深會計師的工作責任很大。妳去看過醫生了嗎？

艾蜜莉：看過了，還看了三次呢。醫生每次都開給我抗生素。有吃藥會覺得好些，但是藥一吃完，就又病了。

瑞　秋：那真慘，而且常吃抗生素對妳身體也不好。

艾蜜莉：我也看過那樣的報導。真希望自己多知道些草本藥方，或其他的另類療法。這個時候我什麼都願意試。

瑞　秋：我也不太懂什麼另類療法，不過妳記不記得我以前常嚴重偏頭痛？

艾蜜莉：當然記得啊！妳每次都沒辦法上班，至少要請個兩天假休養。

瑞　秋：後來我男朋友給我這種叫小白菊的藥草。我不知道他從哪裡買的，不過只要我一覺得偏頭痛快犯了，就吃三片這種草本藥片，一天兩次，頭就不痛了耶，很神奇喔。

艾蜜莉：我不知道有哪一種藥草可以治好我。

瑞　秋：一定有的。妳有沒有聽過紫錐花？我想它可以增強免疫

　　　　　系統，就像一種自然的抗生素。

艾蜜莉：我聽過。妳可不可以問問妳男朋友在哪裡買偏頭痛藥草，

　　　　　我可以去看看那邊有什麼藥適合我。

瑞　秋：好啊，我現在就打給傑生。

語　法

- I haven't seen you in weeks. （我好幾個禮拜沒看到你了。）

  與 I haven't seen you for weeks. 的意思相同。上一句的 in 通常用於否定句，意指在某個期間未做某事。

- How's it going? （最近好嗎?）

  這是日常生活的寒喧用語，通常用於親密的朋友之間。表達方式如同 How are you?，用以問候對方的健康情形或工作是否順利。我們可以回答對方：Fine. / Great! / I'm doing all right.。

- Have you been to see a doctor? （你去看過醫生了嗎?）

  have been to do～的形式是表「已經去做～」之意。Have you been to see a doctor? 的意思即和 Have you seen a doctor? 相同。另舉一個同樣句型的例句：*Have you been to* see the Picasso exhibition yet?（你去看過畢卡索的畫展了嗎?）。

Speaking Function 9

好奇想知道的說法

 請聽《Track 5》。

1. A: I wonder what's in this box.

   B: I have no idea. Do you want to open it?

2. A: I'm curious to know how much it'll cost.

   B: About $2,000.

3. A: I wish I knew more about alternative medicine.

   B: You might want to read this book, then.

解說

● 好奇想知道某件事的常用句型是 I wonder...（我想知道…），wonder 之後可直接加上疑問詞，如 I wonder what's in this box.（真想知道這個箱子裡頭裝什麼東西?），也可接續連接詞 if 或 whether，如 I wonder if/whether she's coming.（我想知道她會不會來?）。

● 「好奇心強的」的英文是 curious，具正面性的意涵。若要表達強烈地想知道某件事，可說 I'm curious to know...。另外，此處的 curious 可用 interested, eager, anxious, fascinated, intrigued 等形容詞替換。

● 想要婉轉表達「真希望自己知道…」時，可用 I wish I knew... 這個假設法過去式的說法。若是要表示「真希望自己知道得更多～」，則說 I wish I knew more about ～，即再加上 more about 兩個字修飾。

練習 1 【代換】

 請隨《Track 6》做代換練習。

1. I wonder *what happened to her.*

                   where they're going on their honeymoon.

                   when she will get married.

                   who is starring in the movie.

                   why he turned down the offer.

                   how he got that position.

2. I'm *curious*　to know how he became successful.

interested
eager
anxious
fascinated
intrigued

3. I wish I knew more about *acupuncture.*

herbal remedies.
aromatherapy.
hypnotherapy.
dietetics.

練習 2【角色扮演】

②請隨《Track 7》在嗶一聲後唸出灰色部分的句子。

1. A: I wonder what's going on in the hall.

　B: I have no idea. Shall we go in and see?

2. A: I'm curious to know how he became so rich.

　B: Well, he made a lot of money in the real estate business.

3. A: I wish I knew more about Chinese cuisine.

　B: My uncle runs a Chinese restaurant. Shall I introduce you
　　 to him?

練習 3【覆誦重要語句】

②請隨《Track 8》覆誦英文句子。

1. in weeks 「好幾個星期」

　↳I've been so busy that I haven't been to the gym in

weeks.（最近好忙，已經好幾個星期沒去體育館運動了。）

2. under the weather 「身體不舒服」
↳When I saw him at the party, he looked a bit under the weather.（我在派對上看到他時，他看起來身體不太好。）

3. have you been to do 「去做過～嗎」
↳"Miss Saigon" is playing at the Broadway Theater. Have you been to see it yet?

（百老匯劇場正在上映『西貢小姐』，你去看過了嗎?）

4. be on (the medicine) 「服（藥）」
↳Linda has been on antidepressants for more than a year.

（琳達已經有一年多持續服用抗鬱劑了。）

5. run out 「用完」
↳Will you talk briefly because time is running out?

（已經沒有什麼時間了，你可不可以長話短說?）

6. at this point 「在這個時候，目前」
↳I haven't read their complaints yet, so I can't comment at this point.

（我還沒看到他們的投訴書，暫時無法提供任何意見。）

7. recover 「復原」
↳Michelle is recovering from a knee injury suffered in a skiing accident.

（蜜雪兒滑雪意外時所受的膝蓋傷正在慢慢復原。）

8. come on 「（疾病等）發作、產生」
↳Let me take a break because I can feel a headache is coming on.（讓我休息一下，我覺得我的頭快痛起來了。）

9. dissipate 「消失」
↳A few minutes after she took the medicine, the pain

dissipated.（在她吃完藥的幾分鐘後，疼痛就消失了。）

10. help out 「幫助」

↳ Nobody helped me out when I was in deep trouble.

（當我深陷困境時，沒有人救助我。）

實力測驗

你從同事那兒聽到有一個人原本罹患胃癌，醫生宣布他活不過一年，但他後來漸漸康復，半年後甚至還出現奇蹟，完全治好癌症。你很好奇他是怎麼痊癒的，請用三種不同的說法詢問同事的看法。

參考解答　　1. I wonder how he overcame his cancer.

2. I'm very curious to know how he overcame his cancer.

3. I wish I knew how he overcame his cancer.

Progress Updates 最新進展

━━━━ Listening ━━━━

Warm-up / Pre-questions

 請聽《Track 9》的新聞報導後回答下面問題。

這段新聞報導傳達的主要訊息是什麼?
- (A) 美國高等教育的水準降低
- (B) 製造業的競爭力降低
- (C) 美國公司內部的員工訓練有良好的成效產生

內容　In a recent study conducted by Manufacturing Data Output (MDO), fewer than 60% of local manufacturers were producing at levels commensurate with overseas producers. This figure is down 14 percent from last year. Unfortunately, the decay has quickened and things are moving from bad to worse. This downturn has resulted in layoffs, closures, and bankruptcies.

Many say that the primary culprit is cheap labor in developing countries. Despite this complaint, tariffs imposed on foreign made products leave a margin for local competition if local manufacturers are technologically prepared to handle it. In another survey conducted by MDO, factory managers complained that the education system does not prepare workers capable of handling the technology vital to the organization's functioning. One respondent commented that out of 100 applications, only 2 to 3 people were capable of learning and operating the company's technology.

中譯　製造業生產資訊機構 (MDO) 最近進行的一項研究指出，只有不到 60% 的本地製造商的生產力能和海外製造商相抗衡。這個數字和去年相比，下滑了14%。不幸的是衰退速度加快，整個情況愈加惡化。這波衰退造成裁員、倒閉、破產的問題。

很多人認為主要原因在於其他發展中國家的廉價勞工。儘管有此抱怨，如果本地製造商已經克服技術問題，準備好要一較長短，在外國商品須課徵關稅的前提之下，本地的競爭產品就仍有生存的空間。MDO 實施的另一項調查顯示，工廠負責人抱怨教育制度未能培養具備公司重要運作技術的人才。其中一名受訪者表示：一百位應徵者裡，只有少數兩、三位有能力學習及運用公司的技術。

解答　(B)

解說　thing 的複數形 things 是表「事情」及「狀況」之意。Things are moving from bad to worse. 是指「情況愈來愈差」，反義則是 Things are getting better.（情況漸漸好轉）。culprit 原義為罪犯，這裡用來隱喻「原因」。despite 是 in spite of（儘管）之意，為報章報導中常出現的字。其他字義：conduct「實施」、manufacturing「製造業的」、output「產量」、local「當地的」、manufacturer「製造業者」、commensurate with「與～程度相當的」、figure「數字」、decay「衰退」、quicken「加速」、move from bad to worse「愈來愈惡化」、downturn「下降」、result in「導致」、closure「停止營業」、bankruptcy「倒閉」、primary「主要的」、labor「勞工」、developing countries「開發中國家」、complaint「抱怨」、tariff「關稅」、impose「課徵」、margin「餘裕」、competition「競爭產品」、vital「要緊的」、respondent「回答者」，而 application 則為「申請」之意。

Listening Step 1

 請聽《Track 10》的會話後回答下面問題。

> 兩個人正在談論什麼事情?
>
> (A) 關於海外銷售網的事情
>
> (B) 關於當地製造廠的事情
>
> (C) 關於雇用外勞的事情
>
> 解答   (B)

Listening Step 2

熟悉下列關鍵字

global   全球的;整體的

production   生產

plant   工廠

productivity   生產力

competitive   具競爭力的

downtime   (機器停止運轉等的)停工期

labor   勞工

computerized technology   電腦化科技

reorganize   重新制定;重新調整

hydraulic robot   液壓自動控制裝置(產業用的機器裝置,用於工廠的機械化生產作業)

exceptional   優秀的

impressive   令人印象深刻的

boost   提高;增加

operate   操作,運作

accomplish   完成,達到

intensive 密集的
last 持續
Vice President of Operations 營運副總裁

2 請聽《Track 11》並在括弧內填入正確答案。

1. I'm pleased with this year's increase in (   ) sales.
2. Can you give me some data on its (   )?
3. We (   ) the budget last year and bought two new hydraulic robots.
4. We have an (   ) group of workers.
5. How did you (   ) that?

解答

1. I'm pleased with this year's increase in (global) sales.
2. Can you give me some data on its (productivity)?
3. We (reorganized) the budget last year and bought two new hydraulic robots.
4. We have an (exceptional) group of workers.
5. How did you (accomplish) that?

2 請再聽一次《Track 10》的會話後回答下面問題。

1. 公司去年購買了什麼東西？
   (A) 大型的電腦
   (B) 生產設備的機器裝置
   (C) 大量的果實
2. 下列哪一項是提高生產力的對策之一？
   (A) 裁員

(B) 延長工作時間

(C) 舉辦密集訓練新技術的課程

Listening Step 3

熟悉下列語句

in comparison to　和～比較

for one thing　首先

invest in　投資於

compensate for　補償

on board　繼續擔任工作團隊中的一員

be scheduled to　預定

boil down to　歸結成

in a nutshell　簡單地說

keep up　保持

② 請聽《Track 12》並在括弧內填入正確答案。

1. I'm concerned about the production of our local plant ( ) ( ) ( ) our overseas plants.

2. ( ) ( ) ( ), sir, it is the new computerized technology that we have invested in locally.

3. Did you lay off workers to ( ) ( ) this purchase?

4. We have an exceptional group of workers and I wanted to keep them all ( ) ( ).

5. So what it ( ) ( ) ( ) is education and

training for the workers.

解答

1. I'm concerned about the production of our local plant (in) (comparison) (to) our overseas plants.
2. (For) (one) (thing), sir, it is the new computerized technology that we have invested in locally.
3. Did you lay off workers to (compensate) (for) this purchase?
4. We have an exceptional group of workers and I wanted to keep them all (on) (board).
5. So what it (boils) (down) (to) is education and training for the workers.

② 請再聽一次《Track 10》的會話後回答下面問題。

---

1. 為什麼不解雇員工?
   (A) 因為勞工工會強烈反對
   (B) 因為員工全部都很優秀
   (C) 因為擔心技術與人才外流

2. 密集訓練課程的特色是什麼?
   (A) 請有名的技術顧問親臨指導
   (B) 員工住在一起集體訓練
   (C) 凡參加者皆有薪水支付

3. 對於營運副總裁的表現,公司總裁給與什麼評價?
   (A) 給與高度的讚賞
   (B) 覺得成績馬馬虎虎、尚可
   (C) 打下低於標準的分數

解答   1. (B)   2. (C)   3. (A)

Speaking

 請再聽一次《Track 10》。

CEO: I'm pleased with this year's increase in global sales, but I'm concerned about the production of our local plant in comparison to our overseas plants. Can you give me some data on its productivity?

Mr. Elton: Yes, sir. I am very happy to say that our local plant produces about 25% of our products, at times and rates competitive with our overseas plants and has very little downtime.

CEO: What seems to be the key to keeping this local plant competitive with our overseas plants when labor is so much cheaper overseas? How are you making this happen?

Mr. Elton: For one thing, sir, it is the new computerized technology that we have invested in locally. We reorganized the budget last year and bought two new hydraulic robots.

CEO: Did you lay off workers to compensate for this purchase?

Mr. Elton: No, sir. We have an exceptional group of workers and I wanted to keep them all on board. I used the hydraulic robots to increase worker productivity by 18%. It is at a 3-year high now.

CEO: Excellent. That is impressive. Is that all that has been done to boost worker productivity?

Mr. Elton: No, actually, sir, the single biggest thing after the hydraulic robot purchase was training the workers to operate more effectively with the new technology.

CEO: How did you accmplish that?

Mr. Elton: I hired instructors and set up an intensive training program that lasted 18 hours. Every employee was scheduled to go to the training and everyone was paid to attend. Productivity improved from the first group of workers to finish the course.

CEO: So what it boils down to is education and training for the workers.

Mr. Elton: Exactly. That's it in a nutshell.

CEO: That sounds like money well spent. I'm impressed with your efforts at this local plant. Without a creative Vice President of Operations such as yourself, this plant would probably be closing soon. Keep up the good work.

Mr. Elton: Thank you, sir. I'll continue to do my best.

中　譯 ⋯⋯⋯⋯⋯⋯⋯⋯⋯⋯⋯⋯⋯⋯⋯⋯⋯⋯⋯⋯⋯⋯⋯⋯⋯⋯⋯⋯

總　裁：我很高興見到我們今年的全球銷售量成長。不過和海外廠相比，我更關心本地廠的生產情況。你可不可以提供一些本地廠的生產力報告？

艾爾頓：好的。我很高興地說本地廠生產了約25%的公司產品，時間上、成本上都和海外廠不相上下，而且很少停工。

總　裁：海外勞工那麼低廉，是什麼要訣能讓本地廠保持和海外廠競爭的實力？你是怎麼做到的？

艾爾頓：是這樣的，首先是我們在本地廠投資了電腦化新科技。去年重新調整預算，購置了兩台新的液壓自動控制裝置。

總　裁：你有用裁員來彌補購買這項裝置的支出嗎？

艾爾頓：沒有。我們的工作小組都很優秀，我想讓他們繼續工作。我利用液壓裝置將員工生產力提高 18%，創了三年來的新高紀錄。

總　裁：太好了，的確令人佩服。就是全靠那個裝置來提昇員工生產力的嗎？

艾爾頓：不是。事實上，還有一件最重要的事，就是在購買液壓裝置後，開始訓練員工如何有效率地運用新技術。

總　裁：怎麼辦到的？

艾爾頓：我請了指導員，並規劃了 18 小時的密集訓練課程，安排每位員工受訓，而且參加訓練的員工都有薪水支付。從第一批員工結訓後，生產力就提高了。

總　裁：所以歸結起來就是員工的教育和訓練。

艾爾頓：沒錯，概括來講是這樣。

總　裁：聽起來錢是用對地方了。我非常滿意你對本地廠的努力經營。如果沒有一位像你這樣有創意的營運副總裁，這家工廠可能再不久就得關閉了。繼續保持工作佳績。

艾爾頓：謝謝您。我會持續全力以赴。

語　法

● in comparison to　（和～比較）

to 可以用 with 替代，說成 in comparison with，如 *In comparison with China, Japan is very small.*（和中國比起來，日本非常小）。也可以用 by 替換 in，說成 by comparison with，如 *By comparison with New York, London is very safe.*（和紐約比起來，倫敦非常安全）。

- at times and rates （在時間上和成本上）

  times 是指投入於生產所花的時間；rates 是指投入於生產所花的費用，即生產成本。

- the single biggest thing （最重大的一件事）

  如 the single most/biggest/greatest，single 置於形容詞的最高級之前，表「真正地」之意，有強調的作用。例句如：The single biggest problem we face is terrorism.（我們所面臨的最大問題正是恐怖主義）。

- money well spent （金錢運用得當）

  money well spent 是強調把錢花在有用的地方，是句慣用語，原為 money was well spent。

Speaking Function 10

歸納、摘要的說法

 請聽《Track 13》。

1. A: So what it boils down to is, nobody wants to take a risk.

   B: I guess so.

2. A: There are no bus or train services at this time of the day.

   B: In other words, we have to take a taxi.

3. A: In a nutshell, then, we have to pay for the damage.

   B: Exactly.

解說

- So what it boils down to is (that)... 是總結之前的談話內容並導入結論的說法。boil 的原義是「沸騰，煮熟」，可引申為把談話內容「濃縮」的意思。「簡要來說就是如下」的英語即是 What it boils down to is this.，其後再接續歸納的要點。

● 要改換字句、重新摘要說明之前的談話內容時，可用 In other words, 表示。除此，也可以使用 So what I'm saying is... / The point I'm making is... / The point I'm trying to make is... 等來摘要總結自己之前的發言。

● 「簡潔地」「總而言之」的英文片語是 in a nutshell / in a word / in short / to sum up。除此之外，也可以用副詞 simply / basically，或用動詞 summarize 來表達。to cut a long story short 則如字面之義所示，是指「長話短說」「簡而言之」的意思。

練習 1【代換】

 請隨《Track 14》做代換練習。

1. So what it boils down to is, *nobody wants to work overtime.*

> I have to do it by myself.
> we have to lay off another 100 workers.
> our funding has been cut.
> they want to cancel the contract.

2. *In other words,*　　　　　　we have to introduce computerized technology immediately.

> So what I'm saying is,
> The point I'm making is,
> The point I'm trying to make is,

3. *In a nutshell, then,* the new computerized technology contributed to the sales increase.

> In a word, then,
> Simply put, then,

To summarize, then,

So basically,

練習 2【角色扮演】

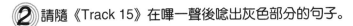 請隨《Track 15》在嗶一聲後唸出灰色部分的句子。

1. A: So what it boils down to is, nobody wants to take the responsibility.

   B: I'm afraid so.

2. A: Our car has given me a lot of trouble recently. The engine overheated the other day and there was also an oil leak.

   B: In other words, we need to buy a new car.

3. A: In a nutshell, then, we cannot avoid a court battle.

   B: Precisely.

練習 3【覆誦重要語句】

請隨《Track 16》覆誦英文句子。

1. in comparison to 「和~比較」

   ↳In comparison to American cars, Japanese cars are far more economical on gas.

   （和美國車比，日本車省油得多。）

2. competitive 「具競爭力的」

   ↳The weak dollar is making domestic goods more competitive in the world market.

   （美元貶值使得美國商品在海外市場更有競爭力。）

3. key 「要訣」

   ↳He thinks the wisdom and power to see into the future is

a key to success.

（他認為成功的要訣是具備洞見未來的智慧和力量。）

4. for one thing 「首先」
   ↳ I don't want to rent this apartment. It's too small for one thing.（我不想租這個公寓，第一個原因就是地方太小了。）

5. compensate for 「補償」
   ↳ Aquaculture is helping to compensate for shrinking supplies of wild fish.

   （水產養殖可以彌補野生漁獲日漸減少的不足。）

6. boost 「提高；增加」
   ↳ The Japanese automaker announced a plan to boost procurements of U.S.-made auto parts. （這家日本汽車製造業者宣布計畫增加採購美製汽車零件。）

7. be scheduled to 「預定」
   ↳ The rock festival is scheduled to take place in Central Park on August 20th.

   （搖滾音樂節預定 8 月 20 日於中央公園舉行。）

8. boil down to 「歸結成」
   ↳ So what it boils down to is, there's still some uncertainty.
   （所以歸納起來，還是存在不確定因素。）

9. in a nutshell 「簡單地說」
   ↳ In a nutshell, he was not suited for the job.
   （總而言之，他不適合這個工作。）

10. keep up 「保持」
    ↳ "Keep up the good work," said the president to Jim.
    （董事長對吉姆說：「繼續保持工作佳績」。）

實力測驗

你的同事吉姆針對企業如何成功不受淘汰的主題做了一番研究，今天他在會議上詳細報告調查結果。聽完報告後，你的心得是：看來企業要在激烈的競爭下生存，就必須要有效率。請你用三種不同的說法表達「簡要來說，要生存就要有效率」的英文。

參考解答

1. So what it boils down to is, we have to streamline to survive.

2. In a nutshell, then, we have to streamline to survive.

3. The point you're making is, we have to streamline to survive.

Stock Prices 股　價

Listening

Warm-up / Pre-questions

 請聽《Track 17》的新聞報導後回答下面問題。

> 投資人對於科技類股股價止跌回升的情形反應如何?
>
> (A) 認為應該立刻進場買股票
>
> (B) 大多認為已經錯失股票的買點
>
> (C) 會猶豫要不要立刻購買股票

內容　XiTech announced Tuesday that the pace of canceled orders had slowed. Many investors took this as a signal that most of the bad news was over for battered tech stocks. As a result, tech stocks extended their winnings to four sessions. XiTech stock increased by 8% causing a boost to other chip stocks as well. PhilConductors, a Philadelphia based semiconductor company's index rallied 7.6% with all 18 of its stocks closing higher. Other tech stocks followed.

The NASDAQ composite index rose 3.6%. The Dow Jones industrials gained 1.3%. The Standard and Poor's 500 index rose 1.5%. Despite this rally, experts disagree on whether the gains will stick. Max Hartford of Hartford & Co. suggested that investors are torn between signs of recovery and the fact that when you see the signs, it's often too late to buy because prices will be higher.

中譯 賽特克科技公司於星期二宣布客戶取消訂單的問題趨緩，很多投資人將這個消息視為徵兆，顯示連日重挫的科技類股已利空出盡。結果，科技類股連續四個交易日拉出長紅，賽特克科技公司股價漲幅為 8%，也帶動其他半導體產業股上漲。費城半導體指數回升了 7.6%，18 支成份股全數收高。其他科技類股也隨之上漲。

那斯達克綜合指數上漲 3.6%，道瓊工業指數上升 1.3%，標準普爾 500 指數上揚 1.5%。儘管股市止跌回升，專家不認為股價會持續上漲。哈特佛公司的麥克斯・哈特佛表示：投資人往往在反彈的跡象出現時拿不定主意，也煩惱若在跡象確立後再出手買就太遲了，因為股價將會漲升一段。

解答 (C)

解說 tech stocks 是 technology stocks 的省略，意指「科技類股」。PhilConductors 由 18 家公司組成，各家股票一同回漲，就形成 index rallied 7.6% with all 18 of its stocks closing higher。the Standard and Poor's 500 index 則是指美國 500 家大企業的股價指數。其他字義：investor「投資人」、signal「徵兆」、battered「受創的」、as a result「結果」、winning「勝利」、session「（證券交易的）市、盤」、boost「提高」、chip stocks「半導體產業股」、based「以～為基地」、semiconductor company「半導體公司」、index「指數」、rally「（價格）回升」、The NASDAQ composite index「那斯達克綜合指數」、The Dow Jones industrials「道瓊工業指數」、Standard and Poor's 500 index「標準普爾 500 指數」、despite「儘管」、gain「（價格）上揚」、stick「持續」、tear「折磨，使精神不安」，而 recovery 為「（價格）反彈」之意。

Listening Step 1

 請聽《Track 18》的會話後回答下面問題。

兩個人正在談論什麼話題?

  (A) 購買股票

  (B) 重建新公司

  (C) 併購其他公司

解答   (A)

Listening Step 2

熟悉下列關鍵字

enthusiastic （對~）熱心的，狂熱的

portfolio 投資組合（投資人持有的有價證券清單）

the profits recession 獲利衰退

exceed 超過

profit decline 利潤減少

judgment 判斷

criteria 標準

nimble 敏捷的

beating 挫折

disciplined 有制度的；有紀律的

flexible 靈活的；有彈性的

lower 降低

spending 花費

cost-cutting measures 降低成本方針

strategic 策略性的

structure 使組織化

buyout　買斷；併購
reasonable　合理的
prospectus　（證券的）公開說明書

 請聽《Track 19》並在括弧內填入正確答案。

1. I am really (　　　　) about the recent market rally.
2. I think that now would be a great time to expand your (　　　) before prices get too high.
3. What are your (　　) for the stock you will select for my portfolio?
4. I will be looking at companies that have become more (　　) through the tech stock beatings.
5. I mean companies that have become more (　　　), more flexible.

解答
1. I am really (enthusiastic) about the recent market rally.
2. I think that now would be a great time to expand your (portfolio) before prices get too high.
3. What are your (criteria) for the stock you will select for my portfolio?
4. I will be looking at companies that have become more (nimble) through the tech stock beatings.
5. I mean companies that have become more (disciplined), more flexible.

 請再聽一次《Track 18》的會話後回答下面問題。

1. McCarthy 先生是怎麼知道股市已經止跌回升的？
   (A) 從網路上得知

(B) 詢問理財顧問後得知

(C) 看了早報後得知

2. McCarthy 先生麻煩跟他通電話的人做什麼事？

(A) 立刻購買科技類股

(B) 傳真公開說明書給他

(C) 晚一點再打電話詳細說明

解答   1. (C)   2. (B)

Listening Step 3

熟悉下列語句

---

wind down   逐漸結束，縮小
I'd say so.   我是這麼認為。
the bulk of   大部分的
in terms of   從～觀點；就～而論
on the upswing   上升，回升
engaged in   從事
have ～ in mind   心裡想～事
be back in touch   再聯絡
within the hour   一小時內
The fax is on the way.   馬上傳真過去。

---

② 請聽《Track 20》並在括弧內填入正確答案。

1. Do you really think that this rally is a sign that the profits recession is (　　　) (　　　)?

2. They are looking for signs that (　　　) (　　　) (　　　) the bad news is over in terms of profit declines.

3. Well, after yesterday's rally, it looks like a lot of people think we're (   ) (   ) (   ).

4. Can you fax me over a quick prospectus on the companies and I will be (   ) (   ) (   ) within the hour?

5. The fax is (   ) (   ) (   ), but remember, we need to move quickly.

解答

1. Do you really think that this rally is a sign that the profits recession is (winding) (down)?

2. They are looking for signs that (the) (bulk) (of) the bad news is over in terms of profit declines.

3. Well, after yesterday's rally, it looks like a lot of people think we're (on) (the) (upswing).

4. Can you fax me over a quick prospectus on the companies and I will be (back) (in) (touch) within the hour?

5. The fax is (on) (the) (way), but remember, we need to move quickly.

② 請再聽一次《Track 18》的會話後回答下面問題。

1. 打電話的人為什麼會主動聯絡 McCarthy 先生?
   (A) 因為要勸誘他買股票
   (B) 因為要拉攏這位新客戶
   (C) 因為要忠告他先不要亂買股票

2. McCarthy 先生認為打電話的人如何?
   (A) 無法令人信賴
   (B) 認為對方的判斷很正確
   (C) 認為對方的意見不夠有說服力

3. 打電話的人希望 McCarthy 先生做什麼決定？

　(A) 迅速展開行動

　(B) 可花一些時間慢慢考慮

　(C) 改換新的理財顧問

解答　　　　　　　　　　　　　　1. (A)　2. (B)　3. (A)

Speaking

會話

 請再聽一次《Track 18》。

Mr. Shell: Hello, Mr. McCarthy. I wanted to give you a call and let you know that I am really enthusiastic about the recent market rally and I think that now would be a great time to expand your portfolio before prices get too high.

Mr. McCarthy: I saw that in the paper this morning. Do you really think that this rally is a sign that the profits recession is winding down?

Mr. Shell: I'd say so. Most investors aren't looking for companies to say that they are going to exceed their last year profits.

Mr. McCarthy: Well then, what are they looking for?

Mr. Shell: They are looking for signs that the bulk of the bad news is over in terms of profit declines.

Mr. McCarthy: Well, after yesterday's rally, it looks like a lot of people think we're on the upswing.

Mr. Shell: Yes, I'd say so. That is why I called you. I am really excited about our ability to get some good prices if we act immediately.

Mr. McCarthy: All right. I trust your judgment. What are your criteria for the stock you will select for my portfolio?

Mr. Shell: I will be looking at companies that have become more nimble through the tech stock beatings.

Mr. McCarthy: What do you mean by "nimble?"

Mr. Shell: I mean companies that have become more disciplined, more flexible — companies that have lowered spending and expanded their cost-cutting measures — engaged in strategic layoffs and structured buyouts.

Mr. McCarthy: That seems reasonable. Do you have any particular companies in mind?

Mr. Shell: Of course. I was thinking of JDS Universal, Lamorex Technologies, Win Systems Incorporated, and Global Software.

Mr. McCarthy: Great. Can you fax me over a quick prospectus on the companies and I will be back in touch within the hour?

Mr. Shell: Sure thing. The fax is on the way, but remember, we need to move quickly.

中　譯 ···

薛　爾：哈囉，麥卡錫先生。我想打電話跟你說，我非常看好最近市場止跌回升，我在想現在是幫你擴大投資組合的好

時機，免得日後股價又漲得太高了。

麥卡錫：今天早上的報紙也這麼說。你真的認為這波止跌回升象徵著企業獲利衰退的情形逐漸結束？

薛　　爾：我是這麼認為。大部分的投資人並不期待企業界宣布今年的營收會多過去年。

麥卡錫：那投資人期待什麼？

薛　　爾：他們期待的是顯示營收衰退的利空消息全部出盡。

麥卡錫：嗯，自從昨天止跌後，好像很多人都認為市場就要回升了。

薛　　爾：是啊，我也這麼認為，這就是為什麼我會打電話給你。如果能馬上採取行動的話，我相信我們能以好價格進場。

麥卡錫：好吧，我相信你的判斷。你幫我篩選投資組合的選股標準是什麼？

薛　　爾：我會注意一些在經歷科技類股挫敗後表現得更敏捷的公司。

麥卡錫：你說「敏捷」是什麼意思？

薛　　爾：我是指那些制度更完備、更靈活變通的公司，能減少開銷、擴大降低成本方案，而且採取策略性裁員、組織性併購的公司。

麥卡錫：聽起來很有道理。你已經想好選擇什麼公司了嗎？

薛　　爾：當然。我在考慮環球JDS公司、拉摩瑞斯科技公司、視窗系統公司，還有全球軟體公司。

麥卡錫：太好了，你可不可以傳真這些公司的概略說明給我，我會在一小時內聯絡你。

薛　　爾：沒問題。馬上就可以傳給你，但是記得我們的動作一定要快。

語 法 ··

- I'd say so. （我是這麼覺得。）

  助動詞 will 的過去式 would 在語感上比原形來得委婉。例如 I'll say so.（我是這麼想）和 I'll say it's too expensive.（我會覺得那樣太貴），皆是一般的斷定句；若改成 I'd say so. 和 I'd say it's too expensive.，則更能帶出說話者態度慎重的語感。

- criteria for （～的標準）

  criteria 是 criterion（標準，尺度）的複數形，必須留意不可使用單數形表示。另「～的標準」講法還須加上介系詞 for。其他常接續 for 的名詞片語包括：aptitude for（～的才能）/ demand for（～的需求）/ remedy for（～的治療）/ substitute for（代替～的人 [物]）等。

- within the hour （一小時以內）

  與 within an hour 的說法相同，必須留意和 in an hour（1 個小時後）的意思不同。

- be on the/its way （馬上好）

  be on the/its way 除了指「在途中」之外，口語上還有「馬上到」的意思。傳真的資料馬上傳到對方手中，即說 The fax is *on the way.*；表示自己立刻到達對方所在地，則是 I'm *on the way.* 或 I'm *on my way.*。

Speaking Function 11

表達興奮、無聊的心情

請聽《Track 21》。

1. A: Did you hear that we are going into the entertainment business?

   B: Yes. I'm very excited about it.

2. A: We're going to Hawaii on our company trip next year.

  B: How exciting!

3. A: What do you think of this TV show?

  B: It's incredibly boring.

解說

● 對於已經發生或即將發生的事感到心情激動、高興地靜不下來時，可用 I'm very excited about/by ～ 表達。例句如：She was very excited about the musical.（這齣音樂劇讓她感到很興奮）/ I'm excited about the coming party.（我很期待即將舉行的派對）。

● 當聽到對方將有不錯的計畫要進行時，可用感嘆句 How exciting! 表達「真棒!」的羨慕心情。除了 exciting 之外，也可以用 wonderful, marvelous, thrilling 等形容詞表達。

● 對於令人厭煩、無法引發內心興趣的事物，我們可以用 It's boring.（真是無聊）表達。若要加以強調，可再補充 incredibly 等的副詞修飾。除此之外，也可以使用 It's a total bore. / It bores me stiff. / It leaves me cold. / It really turns me off. 等慣用說法。

練習 1【代換】

 請隨《Track 22》做代換練習。

  1. *I'm very excited about* the buyout scheme.

     I'm very enthusiastic about
     I'm very fascinated by
     I'm thrilled at
     I can't deny my enthusiasm for

  2. "My uncle said he would get us tickets for Tyson's next bout."

"How exciting!"

"How wonderful!"

"How marvelous!"

"How thrilling!"

3. "What do you think of this exhibition?"

"It's incredibly boring."

"It's a total bore."

"It bores me stiff."

"It leaves me cold."

"It really turns me off."

練習 2【角色扮演】

請隨《Track 23》在嗶一聲後唸出灰色部分的句子。

1. A: Did you know Tom Hanks is coming to the reception?

   B: Yes. I'm very excited about it.

2. A: Our company's 20th anniversary celebration is going to be a dinner cruise onboard a yacht.

   B: How exciting!

3. A: What do you think of this musical?

   B: It's incredibly boring.

練習 3【覆誦重要語句】

請隨《Track 24》覆誦英文句子。

1. now would be a great time to do　「現在是做～的大好時機」

   ↳I think now would be a great time to buy stock of

technology companies.

（我認為現在是買進科技類股的大好時機。）

2. wind down 「逐漸結束，縮小」

↳Most auto companies are winding down production of sports-utility vehicles due to the recession. （由於經濟衰退，大部分的汽車公司慢慢減少生產運動休旅車。）

3. exceed 「超過」

↳John's performance at his new position exceeded my expectation. （約翰接任新職務的表現超出了我的預料。）

4. the bulk of 「大部分的」

↳We have never depended on newspaper advertising for the bulk of our revenues.

（我們從來不靠報紙廣告賺取大部分的收益。）

5. in terms of 「從～觀點；就～而論」

↳Jim is not popular among his colleagues because he thinks of everything in terms of money. （吉姆在同事間的人緣並不好，因為他老愛用金錢衡量事情。）

6. on the upswing 「上升，回升」

↳A recent report indicates that crimes committed by teenagers are on the upswing.

（最近一份報告指出，青少年犯罪案件正在增加中。）

7. criteria 「標準」

↳Criteria for diamond quality consist of cut, carat weight, clarity, and color. （鑽石品質的判斷標準包含切割技巧、克拉重量、淨度，以及色澤。）

8. have ～ in mind 「心裡想～事」

↳It's a good idea to celebrate our successful joint venture

tonight. Do you have any particular place in mind? (今晚來慶祝我們合資成功的點子很棒,你有沒有想到什麼特別的好地方?)

9. reasonable 「合理的」
   ↳ It seems reasonable that adolescents who commit violent crimes should be tried as adults. (犯下重罪的青少年應同成年人受同樣的審判,這點似乎很合理。)

10. be in touch with 「跟~聯絡」
   ↳ I'll be in touch with you again about this matter when I come back from San Francisco.
   (關於這件事,我從舊金山回來後會再跟你聯絡。)

實力測驗

公司宣布要派你到英國倫敦出差。由於你沒去過倫敦,所以內心感到非常興奮。有一位知道這個消息的同事跑來對你說: I heard you're going to London on business. (聽說你要到倫敦出差),這時你會如何表達興奮的心情呢? 請用三種不同的說法回答。

參考解答 1. Yes. I've never been there and I'm very excited about it.
2. Yes. It's going to be my first trip there and I'm already thrilled at it.
3. Yes. I've always wanted to go there so I can't deny my enthusiasm for the trip.

Chapter
12
A New Product
新產品

Listening

Warm-up / Pre-questions

 請聽《Track 25》的廣告後回答下面問題。

什麼樣的人會最需要這段廣告介紹的新產品?
(A) 經常賴床的人
(B) 經常到國內外各地旅行的人
(C) 在意指針走動的聲音而失眠的人

內容 Is time important to you? Do you like to be on time? Do you travel a lot? If you answered "yes" to any of these questions, you will be excited to learn about the new craze in timekeeping —radio-controlled watches. Gone are the days when you have to keep resetting your watch for accuracy, daylight saving time, and time zone shifts. Radio-controlled watches automatically synchronize with the National Institute of Standards and Technology's radio signal. In other words, these timepieces adjust themselves for standard or daylight saving, change within one hour to any world time, and are impeccably accurate as a result of automatic daily resets.

These watches come in a variety of stylish designs with built-in antennas for the time signal. Most are waterproof and shock-resistant with an average battery life of 3 years. If you are up for a change in time, try out an atomic wristwatch. They are usually available in any upscale store that sells fine Swiss watches or on the Internet by typing the keywords, "radio-controlled watches."

中譯　時間對你而言重要嗎？你喜歡準時嗎？你經常旅遊嗎？如果上述任一問題，你的答案為「是」的話，你會很樂於知道現今錶的最新潮流——電波手錶。從前為求精準、或遇日光節約時間、時差等而不斷調手錶時間的問題，都將成為過去式。電波手錶會自動和美國國家標準與技術研究院的無線電訊號對時。換言之，這種手錶可以自動調成標準時間或日光節約時間，一小時內更改為各地時間，並且由於每日自動重設而完美精準。

電波手錶有多種風格設計，具內建對時天線，大部分都防水防震，電池壽命平均三年。如果你打算不久後更換品味，不妨試試原子腕表，各大高級瑞士鐘錶店均有販售，或上網搜尋關鍵字「電波手錶」，都能買得到。

解答　(B)

解說　Gone are the days when... 這句話運用了倒裝句的手法，原本為 The days when...are gone，意指「…的時代已經過去（結束）了」。 If you are up for a change in time 的 be up for 是「有意於」、a change 是「改變」、in time 則是「將來」之意，整個子句解釋為「若不久後打算換買新的」。其他字義: on time「準時地」、craze「大流行」、timekeeping「守時」、radio-controlled watches「電波手錶，無線電控制的手錶」、accuracy「正確（性）」、daylight saving time「日光節約時間」、time zone「時區」、synchronize「使一致」、the National Institute of Standards and Technology「美國國家標準與技術研究院」、timepiece「錶」、adjust「調整」、impeccably「完美地」、accurate「準確的」、built-in「內建的」、time signal「報時信號」、waterproof「防水的」、shock-resistant「耐震的」、battery life「電池壽命」、try out「充分試驗」、atomic wristwatch「原子腕錶（電波手錶的別稱）」、upscale store「高級

店」，而 fine 為「精巧的」之意。

Listening Step 1

 請聽《Track 26》的會話後回答下面問題。

對話中的 Peter 和 Bob 兩人是什麼身分？

 (A) 鐘錶店的顧客

 (B) 鐘錶店的店員

 (C) 一起經營鐘錶店的老闆

解答   (B)

Listening Step 2

熟悉下列關鍵字

redeye 夜航班機

Wow. 哇!（表示驚訝、喜悅、痛苦等的叫聲）

neat 絕佳的

good thinking 設想周到；判斷正確

leather strap 皮帶

face 面板

lecture 演講，講解

prospective customer 潛在的顧客

evolution 演進

mechanical 機械的

electronic 電子的

interested customer 有興趣的客戶

adjustment 調整

admit　承認

conversation piece　引起對話的話題

write-up　報導

one-page　一頁的

summary　摘要

revolution　革命；大變革

wrist　手腕

② 請聽《Track 27》並在括弧內填入正確答案。

1. I took a (　　) to Minnesota Friday night.

2. I really like that Maximum style with the black leather (　　) and white face.

3. I have to admit knowing the watches history is a nice conversation (　　).

4. Where is the history (　　) so I know what I am talking about?

5. Mr. Cable printed this one-page (　　) for us to become familiar with.

解答

1. I took a (redeye) to Minnesota Friday night.

2. I really like that Maximum style with the black leather (strap) and white face.

3. I have to admit knowing the watches history is a nice conversation (piece).

4. Where is the history (write-up) so I know what I am talking about?

5. Mr. Cable printed this one-page (summary) for us to become familiar with.

② 請再聽一次《Track 26》的會話後回答下面問題。

1. Bob 在哪裡度週末?
   (A) 自己的家中
   (B) 明尼蘇達
   (C) 位於芝加哥的 Cable 先生的別墅
2. Peter 想買什麼款式的手錶?
   (A) 價格低於 130 美元的電波手錶
   (B) 黑色面板、褐色錶帶的電波手錶
   (C) 白色面板、黑色錶帶的電波手錶

解答   1. (B)   2. (C)

Listening Step 3

熟悉下列語句

get to do   可以去做
in action   在運作中
on sale   拍賣中
line up   安排；準備
look forward to   期待
keep a person informed   持續提供某人最新的詳細資訊
become familiar with   精通於；熟悉

② 請聽《Track 28》並在括弧內填入正確答案。

1. I actually got to see my new radio-controlled watch (   )
   (   ).

2. I've been waiting to buy one until this week when we put

them (　　　) (　　　) here in the store.
3. He even has a little lecture (　　　) (　　　).
4. Mr. Cable wants us to (　　　) the customers (　　　).
5. Mr. Cable printed this one-page summary for us to (　　　)
(　　　) (　　　).

解答
1. I actually got to see my new radio-controlled watch (in) (action).
2. I've been waiting to buy one until this week when we put them (on)
(sale) here in the store.
3. He even has a little lecture (lined) (up).
4. Mr. Cable wants us to (keep) the customers (informed).
5. Mr. Cable printed this one-page summary for us to (become) (familiar)
(with).

② 請再聽一次《Track 26》的會話後回答下面問題。

1. Bob 為什麼搭乘夜航班機？
(A) 因為要欣賞美麗的夜景
(B) 因為要趕回來準備上班
(C) 因為只能訂到晚上飛機的機位

2. 對於必須向顧客詳細說明電波手錶的事，Peter 有何看法？
(A) 認為沒有說明的必要
(B) 理應主動為客戶詳細說明
(C) 認為可以獲得顧客的信賴

3. 電波手錶的簡介是為了什麼目的所準備？
(A) 為了發給顧客做宣傳
(B) 為了刊載在網路上

(C) 為了讓店員充分瞭解這項新產品

解答　　　　　　　　　　　　　1. (B)　2. (A)　3. (C)

Speaking

會話

 請再聽一次《Track 26》。

Bob: Good morning, Peter. How was your weekend?

Peter: Great, Bob. It was too short, though. How was yours?

Bob: Really good. I took a redeye to Minnesota Friday night and another redeye last night to get back in time for work.

Peter: Wow. That's a lot of traveling for the weekend. Minnesota is two hours ahead of us, too. That's a time zone shift.

Bob: Yes, I know. I actually got to see my new radio-controlled watch in action. It's really neat the way it automatically synchronizes with the new time wherever you travel.

Peter: I know. I've been waiting to buy one until this week when we put them on sale here in the store.

Bob: That's good thinking. All radio-controlled watches are 15% off this week.

Peter: I really like that Maximum style with the black leather strap and white face. It's only $130 with the 15% discount.

Bob: I know. These watches are really a good deal. Mr. Cable is expecting us to sell plenty of them this week, too. He even has a little lecture lined up that we're supposed to give prospective customers about the evolution of the watch from mechanical to electronic to radio-controlled.

Peter: You must be kidding! Am I expected to give a history lecture on these watches to every interested customer?

Bob: I'm afraid so, Peter. You know how Mr. Cable is on customer service and client interaction. I'm not looking forward to it, either.

Peter: These watches are so incredible with their automatic adjustment to daylight saving time and different time zones, plus their automatic daily resets, they should sell themselves without a history lecture!

Bob: You would think so, but Mr. Cable wants us to keep the customers informed. I have to admit knowing the watches history is a nice conversation piece.

Peter: If Mr. Cable insists, I suppose I've got to do it, then. Where is the history write-up so I know what I am talking about?

Bob: Here. Mr. Cable printed this one-page summary for us to become familiar with. I suggest you read it now.

Peter: "The Revolution on Your Wrist," sounds interesting. I'll read it now so I will be prepared when the first customer arrives.

包柏：早安，彼得。週末過得如何？

彼得：很好，包柏。可惜時間太短了。你呢？

包柏：過得很棒。星期五晚上我搭了夜航班機去明尼蘇達，昨晚
又搭晚班機回來準備上班。

彼得：哇喔！短短的週末就跑這麼遠啊。明尼蘇達也比這裡快兩
個鐘頭，有時差上的不同呢。

包柏：是啊，我知道。我其實是要試試我的新電波手錶功能如何。
不論到哪裡，它都自動和當地時間對時，真是太好用了。

彼得：我了解。我一直想買，但我要等到這禮拜我們店裡打折，
才會買一支。

包柏：想得真周到。這禮拜所有電波手錶都打 85 折。

彼得：我真的很喜歡那款黑色錶帶白色面板多功能型的錶，打完
85 折只要 130 美元。

包柏：我知道，買這些錶真的很划算。蓋伯先生也希望我們這禮
拜能多賣出一些。他甚至準備了一些說明內容要我們解說
給有意購買的顧客聽，講解手錶從機械到電子再到無線電
控制的發展過程。

彼得：你一定在開玩笑吧！我得對每個有興趣的客人都講解一次
這些手錶的歷史？

包柏：恐怕是真的，彼得。你也知道蓋伯先生非常重視顧客服務
和與顧客的互動關係。我也不希望講那些東西。

彼得：這些錶具有依日光節約時間和不同時區自動對時的神奇功
能，再加上每天自動重新設定，就算沒有說明發展的歷史，
應該還是可以賣得很好。

包柏：你這樣想沒錯，可是蓋伯先生希望我們隨時提供顧客所有的資訊。我必須承認知道手錶的背景是個開啟話匣子的好題材。

彼得：如果蓋伯先生堅持的話，我想我只好照辦了。說明稿在哪裡？我看了才知道要說什麼。

包柏：在這裡。蓋伯先生印了這一頁簡介，讓我們了解背景。我建議你現在就讀。

彼得：「手腕上的大變革」聽起來蠻有趣的。我現在就開始讀，等第一位客人來的時候，我就準備妥當了。

語　法

● two hours ahead of us　（比這裡快兩個鐘頭）
　ahead 除了表示位置、方向的「在前」之外，也表示時間上的「在前」。由於美國自東海岸到西海岸共有三個時區，所以對住在洛杉磯的人來說，New York is three hours ahead of us.（紐約比我們快三個鐘頭）；反之，對紐約來說則是 Los Angeles is three hours behind us.（洛杉磯比我們慢三個鐘頭）。另外，將鐘調快一個小時的說法是 set the clock ahead one hour，調慢一個小時則是 set the clock back one hour。

● keep the customers informed　（持續提供顧客最新的詳細資訊）
　keep a person informed 意指「持續提供某人最新的詳細資訊」，著重在隨時不間斷地提供事情的發展。若想要隨時知道一件事的最新資訊，可向對方說 Keep me informed of the progress.（讓我知道所有最新的進展）。

● I suggest you read it now.　（我建議你現在就讀。）
　這是假設法現在式的句子。美式英語在表建議、要求、命令等的動詞之後所接續的名詞子句中會運用假設法現在式，即在名詞子句中使用動詞的原形。所以儘管將句中的 you 改成 he，也是使用原形，即 I suggest he read it now.，並不須特意改成第三人稱單數現在式 reads。

另外，當我們將句中的 suggest 改用過去式表達時，後面的 read 也是用原形即可，如 I suggested he read it now.，也不須改成過去式（read 的過去式同樣為 read [rɛd]）。

Speaking Function 12

詢問是否必須做以及回答必須做

請聽《Track 29》。

1. A: Am I expected to complete the report by Thursday?
   B: I'm afraid so, Jim.
2. A: Am I required to put on a tie and a jacket?
   B: Yes, the reception is very formal.
3. A: I don't really have to attend the meeting, do I?
   B: I'm afraid you've got to.

解說

● expect 除了「期待」之意外，亦表「（理當如此的）要求」，當要委婉客氣地詢問「我必須做～嗎?」時，可用 Am I expected to ～? 來表達。

●「我必須做～嗎?」的表達方式除了 Am I expected to ～? 之外，還有 Am I required to ～? / Am I supposed to ～? / Do I really have to ～? / Do I really need to ～? / Must I ～? / Have I got to ～? 等等。最後的 Have I got to ～? 是簡略的口語說法。

● 要向對方表示「你必須做～」時，可以用 You've got to ～來表達，而開頭若再加上 I'm afraid 的話，語氣上會顯得更委婉。除 You've got to ～之外，還可以用 I'm afraid you ought to ～ / I'm afraid you must ～ / I'm afraid you can't avoid ～等等的說法表達。

練習 1【代換】

 請隨《Track 30》做代換練習。

1. Am I expected to *go to a karaoke bar with the client?*

    make a speech at the wedding ceremony?
    bring my own laptop?
    show my ID card at the gate?
    return the car by 3 o'clock?

2. *Am I required to*   buy accident insurance?

    Am I supposed to
    Do I really have to
    Do I really need to
    Must I
    Have I got to

3. "I don't really have to make a speech at the reception, do I?"

    "*I'm afraid you've got to.*"

    "I'm afraid you ought to."

    "I'm afraid you must."

    "I'm afraid you can't avoid it."

練習 2【角色扮演】

 請隨《Track 31》在嗶一聲後唸出灰色部分的句子。

1. A: Am I expected to turn off my cellular phone here?

    B: I'm afraid so, sir.

2. A: Am I required to make a donation?

    B: Not really, but if you do, it would be very nice.

3. A: I don't really have to participate in the workshop, do I?

   B: I'm afraid you've got to.

練習 3【覆誦重要語句】

 請隨《Track 32》覆誦英文句子。

  1. redeye 「夜航班機」

    ↳I took a redeye to New York late Sunday so that I could attend the Monday morning meeting at the headquarters. （上星期日我搭夜航班機到紐約，以便參加星期一早上在總公司舉辦的會議。）

  2. get to do 「可以去做」

    ↳Did you get to meet Mr. Wagner while you were in Philadelphia?（你在費城的時候有見到華格納先生嗎?）

  3. in action 「在運作中」

    ↳Could I see the latest videoconferencing system in action?

    （我可不可以看看最新的視訊會議系統實際的運作情形?）

  4. synchronize with 「使和～一致」

    ↳The sophisticated machine electronically synchronizes the sound with the actors' lip movements.（這台精密的電子機器能將聲音和演員的嘴唇動作配合起來。）

  5. on sale 「拍賣中」

    ↳I bought this radio-controlled watch on sale at Sears last week.（這只電波手錶是我上星期在席爾斯百貨特價的時候買的。）

  6. off 「折價」

↳ The store is closing and everything there is up to 60% off. （這家店即將關閉，每件商品最高打到 4 折。）

7. line up　「準備（活動等）」
↳ There are a lot of interesting events lined up for the annual Sea and Sky Festival.

（年度海空慶典中安排了許多有趣的活動。）

8. keep a person informed　「持續提供某人最新的詳細資訊」
↳ Mr. Conaway told his secretary to keep him informed of the accident that took place at the New Jersey plant.

（康那威先生要秘書隨時讓他知道紐澤西廠意外的最新消息。）

9. write-up　「報導」
↳ This booklet contains a short write-up of each hotel and restaurant in town.

（這本小冊子裡有鎮上每家飯店及餐廳的簡短介紹。）

10. become familiar with　「精通於；熟悉」
↳ Reading the business and finance sections of the newspaper will help you become familiar with the terms used in the marketplace.

（多讀報紙的財經版可以讓你熟悉商業界的習慣用語。）

實力測驗

你到一家汽車出租店租車，辦完租借手續後，店員對你說要麻煩你在還車之前加滿油。你在想真的有必要那樣做嗎？請用三種不同的說法表達內心的疑問。

1. Am I really expected to fill up the tank before I return the car?
2. Am I really supposed to fill up the tank before I return the car?
3. Do I really have to fill up the tank before I return the car?

Chapter 13

Investment Portfolio 投資組合

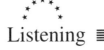

Listening

Warm-up / Pre-questions

 請聽《Track 33》的新聞報導後回答下面問題。

下列哪一項為本篇新聞報導的內容？
(A) Webmonitor 公司的股價暴跌
(B) Webmonitor 公司的總裁表示該公司可能無法達成預期收益
(C) 分析師指出 Webmonitor 公司將被競爭對手收購

內容　CEO John Backer said Tuesday that Webmonitor Ltd. will meet earnings expectations for the next quarter despite the recent share price dive of 59 cents per share. While stockholders' buying patterns cause fluctuations in share prices, customers are still purchasing Webmonitor products.
Backer commented, "While we are encouraged by sales, we believe there is much more work to be done." Analysts expect the customer base to shrink by about 2% this next quarter. This means that Webmonitor has to turn around in a tightening market. Webmonitor expects to meet these demands by job cuts and sales of subsidiary businesses such as its 4,300 worker fiber cable business.

中譯　網路觀測公司總裁約翰貝克週二表示，儘管最近每股股價大跌 59 美分，網路觀測公司還是會達到下一季的預期收益。雖然持股人的買賣行為導致股價波動，顧客仍持續購買網路觀測公司

的產品。

貝克說：「雖然銷售成績鼓舞了我們的信心，我們認為仍有許多工作必須努力去完成。」分析師預測客戶基礎將於今年下一季縮減 2%，這代表網路觀測公司必須在日漸緊縮的市場反轉逆勢。為了達成這些需求，網路觀測公司將減少雇用並出售子公司，例如出售擁有 4,300 名員工、從事光纖纜線業務的子公司。

解答　(A)

解說　meet 除了「遇見」之意外，還有「符合」「滿足」要求、期待、條件等之意；meet a person's wishes 是「符合人的期望」、meet demands 是「滿足要求」、meet a condition 則是「符合條件」的意思。本篇新聞報導中的 meet earnings expectations 是「達到預期收益」、meet these demands 是「符合這些要求」之意。單字意思如下：earnings「收益」、expectation「預期」、despite「儘管」、dive「暴跌」、stockholder「持股人，股東」、fluctuation「變動」、shrink「減少」、turn around「（生意等）好轉」、tightening market「緊縮的市場」、job cut「減少雇用」，而 subsidiary business 為「子公司」之意。

Listening Step 1

 請聽《Track 34》的會話後回答下面問題。

這兩位男士正在電話中談論什麼事？

　(A) 該不該賣出目前手邊的股票

　(B) 是否應該再多購買高科技類股的股票

　(C) Webmonitor 公司發出的聲明是否可信

解答　　　　　　　　　　　　　　　　　　　　　　　　　　(A)

Listening Step 2

熟悉下列關鍵字

disturbing	令人心神不寧的
stock portfolio	股票投資組合
particularly	尤其
considerable	相當多的
aggressive	積極的
growth	成長
reality	現實
initial	開始的，初次的
optimistic	樂觀的
comeback	恢復
release	發表
statement	聲明
reiterate	重申
attain	達成
pro forma	估計的
profitability	收益率
recommendation	建議
long-term	長期的
contract	契約
provide	提供
revenue	收入，收益
visibility	明顯性；能見度
patient	有耐心的

② 請聽《Track 35》並在括弧內填入正確答案。

1. I saw a (　　　　) decline in my stock portfolio, particularly

my Webmonitor stock.

2. I'm getting nervous as I see how much of my (   ) investment I have already lost.

3. I'm (   ) that Webmonitor will have a comeback by the end of the quarter.

4. My (   ) is to hold the stock.

5. They are a stable company with many long-term contracts that can (   ) excellent revenue and earnings visibility.

解答

1. I saw a (disturbing) decline in my stock portfolio, particularly my Webmonitor stock.

2. I'm getting nervous as I see how much of my (initial) investment I have already lost.

3. I'm (optimistic) that Webmonitor will have a comeback by the end of the quarter.

4. My (recommendation) is to hold the stock.

5. They are a stable company with many long-term contracts that can (provide) excellent revenue and earnings visibility.

② 請再聽一次《Track 34》的會話後回答下面問題。

1. Webmonitor 公司的股價上個禮拜下跌了多少？
   (A) 3%
   (B) 6%
   (C) 9%

2. 股票經紀人 Harris 先生的建議是什麼？
   (A) 繼續持有 Webmonitor 公司的股票

(B) 立刻賣掉 Webmonitor 公司的股票

(C) 將投資於股票的一半的錢改為投資公債

解答   1. (B)   2. (A)

Listening Step 3

熟悉下列語句

get out　抽身
the reality is (that)...　事實是…
ride out　安然度過
What makes you...?　什麼原因讓你…?
hold on to　繼續保有

② 請聽《Track 36》並在括弧內填入正確答案。

1. I need to know if I should (　　　) (　　　) now before I lose everything.

2. I remember, but the (　　　) (　　　), I'm getting nervous as I see how much of my initial investment I have already lost.

3. You need to learn to (　　　) (　　　) these waves.

4. (　　　) (　　　) (　　　) so certain?

5. So you think that I should (　　　) (　　　) (　　　) the stock?

解答

1. I need to know if I should (get) (out) now before I lose everything.

2. I remember, but the (reality) (is), I'm getting nervous as I see how much

of my initial investment I have already lost.

3. You need to learn to (ride) (out) these waves.

4. (What) (makes) (you) so certain?

5. So you think that I should (hold) (on) (to) the stock?

2 請再聽一次《Track 34》的會話後回答下面問題。

1. John 為什麼打電話給 Harris？

　(A) 因為想問股票賺了多少錢

　(B) 因為自己投資的股票暴跌

　(C) 因為不滿意上星期製作出來的投資組合

2. Harris 對於 Webmonitor 公司的未來發展有何看法？

　(A) 感到不滿意

　(B) 感到悲觀

　(C) 感到樂觀

3. John 後來決定怎麼做？

　(A) 賣掉手邊的股票

　(B) 繼續持有目前的股票

　(C) 直接打電話給 Webmonitor 公司

解答　　　　　　　　　　　　1. (B)　2. (C)　3. (B)

Speaking

會話

 請再聽一次《Track 34》。

Customer: Hi, Mr. Harris. I saw a disturbing decline in my stock portfolio, particularly my Webmonitor stock, and I wanted to call you to see if I should sell now before it goes lower.

Stock Portfolio Manager: Oh, I can see why you might be worried, John. That Webmonitor stock did fall 6% last week.

Customer: Yes. That really scared me. I need to know if I should get out now before I lose everything.

Stock Portfolio Manager: Well, John, I explained to you before we built this portfolio that there was a considerable risk in aggressive growth, high-tech stocks like this.

Customer: I remember, but the reality is, I'm getting nervous as I see how much of my initial investment I have already lost.

Stock Portfolio Manager: John, you need to learn to ride out these waves. I'm optimistic that Webmonitor will have a comeback by the end of the quarter. They just had a bad month.

Customer: What makes you so certain?

Stock Portfolio Manager: Well, they released a statement yesterday reiterating the fact that despite this temporary downturn, they expect to attain pro forma profitability by the end of the quarter.

Customer: So you think that I should hold on to the stock?

Stock Portfolio Manager: John, my recommendation is to hold the stock. They are a stable company with many long-term contracts that can provide excellent revenue and earnings visibility. You just have to be patient.

Customer: Thanks, Mr. Harris. I feel more confident about keeping the stock now.

中 譯 ....

客　戶：嗨，哈理斯先生。我投資的股票全部一直下跌，尤其是網路觀測公司的股票。我想打電話問你，我是不是應該現在賣出，以免又跌得更低。

股票經紀人：喔，約翰，我可以理解你為什麼會擔心。網路觀測的股票上個星期確實跌了 6%。

客　戶：是啊，那真令我擔心。我必須知道是不是應該在賠光本錢之前趕緊抽身。

股票經紀人：約翰，在我們製作投資組合前，我曾向你解釋過投資像這種高成長、高科技類股是有相當大的風險。

客　戶：我記得，可是說實在的，只要一看到我最初投資所損失的數目，我就越來越不安。

股票經紀人：約翰，你必須學著去度過這些起起落落。我還是很看好網路觀測，我相信他們到了季末的時候會再回升，他們只是這個月表現不佳。

客　戶：你怎麼能這麼肯定？

股票經紀人：他們昨天發布一項聲明，重申儘管面臨短期衰退現象，他們預期會在本季結束前達到估計獲利率。

客　戶：所以你認為我應該續抱這些股票?

股票經紀人：約翰，我的建議是持股續抱。他們是一家穩定的公
　　　　　　司，簽了許多長期合約，而那些合約能提供豐厚的收益，
　　　　　　利潤也是可以預見的。你只是需要耐心一點。

客　戶：謝謝，哈理斯先生。現在我對這些持股比較有信心了。

語　法 ....

● see　（確認，查看）

　　see 的基本義為「看，看見」，另外可以接續 wh- 子句或 if, whether 等
　連接詞，用於表示「確認」「查看」之意。例句如：*See* who's at the door.
　（去看看誰在門外）/ I'll *see* if he left a message for you.（我會確認他
　有沒有留言給你）。

● What makes...?　（什麼原因…? 為什麼…?）

　　使役動詞 make 有「使（人等）做…」之意。利用 make 所造的疑問
　句：What makes + 人，則意指「什麼原因讓（人）…，（人）為什麼
　…」。因此，例如 Why did you come here? 的句子，可替換成 *What made*
　you come here?（什麼風把你給吹來了?），而 Why are you so nervous?
　也可改為 *What makes* you so nervous?（什麼原因讓你這麼緊張?）。

Speaking Function 13

表達樂觀與悲觀的說法

 請聽《Track 37》。

1. A: I'm very optimistic that we'll be able to finish this job in a
　　 week.

　 B: I certainly hope so.

2. A: I'm very nervous about my audition.

   B: Don't worry. Everything'll be fine.

3. A: What are the prospects of reaching an agreement at today's meeting?

   B: To tell the truth, I'm not all that optimistic about it.

解說

● 對於某件事的看法是樂觀時，可用 I'm optimistic about～或 I'm optimistic + that 子句的說法表達。「我對此感到樂觀」的英文是 I'm optimistic about it.；「我有信心景氣會馬上回升」則是 I'm optimistic that business will pick up soon.。

● 看到朋友為一件事煩惱到垂頭喪氣時，可以說 Everything'll be fine. / It'll all turn out fine. / It'll all turn out OK. 來為他加油打氣；也可以在這些句子之前再加上 Don't worry.，更能充分表達安慰之情。另外，對於擔心考試的人，可以用 I feel quite sure you'll succeed. 或 I don't see how you can fail. 的激勵句。

● 對於事情的發展抱持悲觀時，可用 I'm not all that optimistic about it. / I'm fairly pessimistic about it. / I'm rather skeptical about it. / I rather doubt it. 等等的說法表達。這些句子之前，也可以再接續如 To tell the truth / I have to say / To be honest / I don't want to sound pessimistic 等語句，強烈表達個人的看法。

練習 1 【代換】

 請隨《Track 38》做代換練習。

1. I'm very optimistic that *he can pass the audition.*

> business will pick up soon.
>
> we'll get a green light for this project.

we'll reach an agreement this time.

the company's stock will go up by the end of the summer.

2. "I'm very nervous about my job interview."

"*Don't worry. Everything'll be fine.*"

"Don't worry. It'll all turn out fine."

"Don't worry. It'll all turn out OK."

"Don't worry. I feel quite sure you'll succeed."

"Don't worry. I don't see how you can fail."

3. "What are the prospects of getting the company back on its feet in a year?"

"*To tell the truth, I'm not all that optimistic about it.*"

"I have to say, I'm fairly pessimistic about it."

"To be honest, I'm rather skeptical about it."

"I don't want to sound pessimistic, but I rather doubt it."

練習 2【角色扮演】

 請隨《Track 39》在嗶一聲後唸出灰色部分的句子。

1. A: I'm very optimistic that we'll be able to catch our plane.

   B: I certainly hope so.

2. A: I'm very nervous about my presentation.

   B: Don't worry. Everything'll be fine.

3. A: What are the prospects of clearing off the debts in a year?

   B: To tell the truth, I'm not all that optimistic about it.

練習 3【覆誦重要語句】

② 請隨《Track 40》覆誦英文句子。

1. disturbing 「令人心神不寧的」
   ↳There are disturbing signs that consumers are losing confidence and retail sales are falling.（有消費者失去信心、零售銷售額減少這些令人不安的徵兆出現。）

2. see if... 「看看是否…」
   ↳I'll call and see if he is able to take the kids to the beach this coming Sunday.（我會打個電話問問他這個星期日能不能帶孩子們去海邊玩。）

3. see why... 「了解為什麼…」
   ↳I can see why you are worried about your stock portfolio, but I assure you it is a very good one.（我可以理解你為什麼擔心你的股票投資情形，不過我可以向你保證這項投資組合絕對值得。）

4. get out 「抽身」
   ↳Fortunately I could get out before the stock prices fell.
   （很幸運地，我能在股價下跌前順利抽身。）

5. the reality is (that)... 「事實是…」
   ↳He keeps saying it is a promising company, but the reality is (that) the company is having difficulties.（他一直說這家公司大有可為，但事實是這家公司經營不順。）

6. comeback 「恢復」
   ↳Thanks to the economic recovery, tourism is making a comeback to our island.
   （拜經濟復甦所賜，我們島上的旅遊業正慢慢恢復。）

7. What makes you...? 「什麼原因讓你⋯?」
   ↳ What makes you so pessimistic about the new venture in India? (什麼原因讓你對印度的新投資這麼悲觀?)

8. reiterate 「重申」
   ↳ The Japanese baseball player reiterated his desire to play in the major leagues.
   (這名日籍棒球選手重申希望進軍大聯盟。)

9. hold on to 「繼續保有」
   ↳ Hold on to the stock because it will appreciate considerably. (不要賣掉手上的股票,它會再漲許多。)

10. recommendation 「建議」
    ↳ My recommendation is to sell the stock right now and buy U.S. dollars. (我的建議是,現在賣股票,改買美元。)

實力測驗

你是一位股票經紀人,有一位客戶針對他是否能從股票重新獲利而問你 What are the prospects of an earnings recovery?,請你用三種表示悲觀意見的說法回答。

參考解答
1. To tell the truth, I'm not all that optimistic about it.
2. I have to say, I'm fairly pessimistic about it.
3. To be honest, I'm rather skeptical about it.

Chapter 14

Sales Report 銷售報告

Listening

Warm-up / Pre-questions

 請聽《Track 41》的廣告後回答下面問題。

下列哪一項非廣告中出現的內容?
(A) 每月 36.50 美元可通話 3,000 分鐘的新優惠方案
(B) 免費提供最新款的行動電話
(C) 擴大長途通話區域,費用比照市內電話費率計算

內容　Anderson Wireless announces its new calling plan that gives you 3,000 minutes a month! That's right! You can talk all you want with this new calling plan. You get 1,500 night and weekend minutes, 1,000 mobile to mobile minutes and 500 anytime minutes all for just $36.50 a month!

Our new plan also includes an extended calling area. You can call to or from 14 Western states for the same price as a local call. This new plan can't be beat! To make the deal even better, we offer our first time customers state-of-the-art Audiovox 185 cellular phones for only $32.50 with a one-year servicing agreement.

Call Anderson Wireless at 1–800–889–9090, stop by one of our 15 locations, or visit us on the web at www. andersonwireless.com and sign up today.

中譯　安德森無線電話公司實施通話計費新方案,每月給你 3,000 分

鐘! 沒錯! 這項特惠新方案讓你愛怎麼打就怎麼打。夜間及週末通話 1,500 分鐘，手機互打 1,000 分鐘，剩餘 500 分鐘於任何時間都可撥打，每月只要 36.50 美元!

我們的新方案也包含擴大通話區域，與西部 14 個州通話的費用和市內電話費一樣。這項新方案無懈可擊! 更物超所值的是，我們將提供最先進的 Audiovox 185 手機加上一年的通話服務給第一次簽訂契約的新客戶，只要 32.50 美元。

今日立即簽訂! 請撥安德森無線公司電話 1-800-889-9090，或親臨我們 15 個服務點，也可以上網 www.andersonwireless.com 瞭解詳情。

解答　(B)

解說　for just $36.50 和 for only $32.50 中出現的 for 是表示「與～交換，以～價格代價」之意，用於以物易物或買賣物品時，例句如 I paid $300 for this jacket. 或 I bought the laptop for $2,000.。calling plan 是「通話方案」、mobile to mobile 是「手機互打」、state-of-the-art 是「(科技等產品)最先進的」、a one-year servicing agreement 是「一年的通話契約」、stop by 是「順道經過」，而 sign up 是「簽訂契約」的意思。

Listening Step 1

 請聽《Track 42》的會話後回答下面問題。

這兩位男士談論的主要話題是什麼?

(A) 通話計費新方案實施後的銷售情形

(B) 最新款手機的銷售情形和消費者的購買反應

(C) 夾頁廣告單的版面設計

解答　(A)

Listening Step 2

熟悉下列關鍵字

due 到期的；應提出的
briefing 簡報
stand 處於～狀態
consistently 一直；一貫地
acquire 獲得
district 區域
enroll 登記
existing customers 現有客戶，舊客戶
convert 變換
prediction 預測，預言
corporate office 主管會議室
base 根據
probability 機率；可能性
full-color 全彩的
flyer insert 夾頁廣告傳單
promising 有希望的
cellular phone 手機
top sales 最高銷售額
award 獎
hopefully 順利的話

②請聽《Track 43》並在括弧內填入正確答案。

1. Oh, I didn't think that report was (   ) for a few months.
2. I just wanted to get a quick (   ) from you so I have an idea of where we stand.
3. In our district, 5,247 new customers have (   ) in the last

two months.

4. What are your (　　　　) for the future, Kevin?

5. What are you basing the (　　　　) on?

解答

1. Oh, I didn't think that report was (due) for a few months.

2. I just wanted to get a quick (briefing) from you so I have an idea of where we stand.

3. In our district, 5,247 new customers have (enrolled) in the last two months.

4. What are your (predictions) for the future, Kevin?

5. What are you basing the (probability) on?

② 請再聽一次《Track 42》的會話後回答下面問題。

1. 通話計費新方案實施後，銷售額在兩個月內上升了多少？

　　(A) 13 %

　　(B) 30 %

　　(C) 35 %

2. Kevin 期待總銷售額可以增加到多少？

　　(A) 13 %

　　(B) 30 %

　　(C) 38 %

解答　　　　　　　　　　　　　　　　　1. (A)　2. (C)

Listening Step 3

熟悉下列語句

---

stop in　順道經過

off the top of one's head　立即（不必想）就能說出的

according to　根據

let's see　讓我想想；嗯…

that is　也就是說

kick in　開始

pull off　贏得（獎項）

---

②　請聽《Track 44》並在括弧內填入正確答案。

1. Thanks for (　　) (　　) to see me today.

2. Well, (　　) (　　) (　　) of my head, sales appear to be increasing consistently.

3. (　　) (　　), what do you expect to see by the time the sales report is due to the corporate office in October?

4. Well, the new advertising campaign (　　) (　　) a month ago.

5. With some hard work in these next few months, hopefully we'll be able to (　　) (　　) (　　) again.

解答

1. Thanks for (stopping) (in) to see me today.

2. Well, (off) (the) (top) of my head, sales appear to be increasing consistently.

3. (That) (is), what do you expect to see by the time the sales report is due to the corporate office in October?

4. Well, the new advertising campaign (kicked) (in) a month ago.

5. With some hard work in these next few months, hopefully we'll be able to (pull) (that) (off) again.

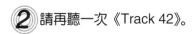 請再聽一次《Track 42》的會話後回答下面問題。

1. Kevin 為什麼回到自己的辦公室？
   (A) 想起有急事要辦
   (B) 為了要拿分析資料
   (C) 為了要拿蒐集好的資料

2. 下列哪一項有助於獲得新客戶？
   (A) 全國統一的通話費率
   (B) 報紙的夾頁廣告傳單
   (C) 在西岸主要都市舉辦宣傳活動

3. 為什麼 Kevin 和他的主管想要贏得區域銷售獎？
   (A) 因為得獎後，可以拿到紅利獎金
   (B) 因為有助於快速升遷
   (C) 因為可以獲得比其他同事多的有給薪假

解答   1. (C)   2. (B)   3. (A)

Speaking

會話

請再聽一次《Track 42》。

Supervisor: Good afternoon, Kevin. Thanks for stopping in to see me today.

Kevin: Good afternoon to you, too, sir. What can I do for you?

Supervisor: Well, Kevin, I was wondering how sales of the new calling plan are going.

Kevin: Oh, I didn't think that report was due for a few months.

Supervisor: You're right, Kevin. It's not due until October, but I just wanted to get a quick briefing from you so I have an idea of where we stand.

Kevin: I see. Well, off the top of my head, sales appear to be increasing consistently. Let me run to my office and grab the data I've been collecting.

Supervisor: Okay. I'll wait for you.

(*A few minutes later, Kevin returns.*)

Kevin: According to this morning's data, sales have increased 13% over the last two months as a direct result of the new calling plan.

Supervisor: That's not bad. How many new customers have we acquired?

Kevin: In our district, 5,247 new customers have enrolled in the last two months.

Supervisor: Good. How many existing customers have converted to the new calling plan?

Kevin: Let's see, about 32%.

Supervisor: What are your predictions for the future, Kevin? That is, what do you expect to see by the time the sales report is due to the corporate office in October?

Kevin: I hope to see a total sales increase of about 38%.

Supervisor: I'd like to see that, too. What are you basing the probability on?

Kevin: Well, the new advertising campaign kicked in a month ago. Every local Sunday paper has a full-color flyer insert. This is usually very effective in drawing in new customers.

Supervisor: That sounds promising.

Kevin: Yes, I think so, sir. Especially since we're offering the newest cellular phone for only $32.50 with a one-year contract. That really can't be beat.

Supervisor: Kevin, you know that I'm hoping for top sales so we can win the district award again. That means a bonus not only for me, but for all of the sales representatives as well.

Kevin: Yes, sir. I know. With some hard work in these next few months, hopefully we will be able to pull that off again.

中　譯 ⋯⋯⋯⋯⋯⋯⋯⋯⋯⋯⋯⋯⋯⋯⋯⋯⋯⋯⋯⋯⋯⋯⋯⋯⋯⋯⋯⋯⋯⋯⋯

主管：午安，凱文。謝謝你特地過來。

凱文：午安，先生。請問您找我有什麼事嗎？

主管：嗯，凱文。我想知道通話計費新方案的銷售情況如何？

凱文：喔，我以為那份報告是再過幾個月才要交。

主管：是沒錯，凱文，十月再交就可以了，不過我只是想聽你作個簡報，好讓我對目前的情形有個概念。

凱文：我懂了。現在可以立即回答的是，銷售額持續增加中。請容許我到我的辦公室拿一些蒐集好的資料。

主管：好，我等你。

（幾分鐘後，凱文回來了）

凱文：根據今天早上的資料，過去兩個月來的銷售額已經增加了
　　　13%，這可直接歸功於通話計費新方案。

主管：還不錯。我們贏得多少新客戶？

凱文：過去兩個月來，在我們這區登記的新客戶為 5,247 人。

主管：很好。那舊客戶換新方案的比例有多少？

凱文：嗯…大約 32%。

主管：凱文，你預測未來會怎麼樣？也就是說，到十月提交銷售
　　　報告給公司的時候，你預期會看到什麼成果？

凱文：我希望總銷售額能成長 38% 左右。

主管：我也希望。你預估的根據是什麼？

凱文：嗯，新的廣告宣傳活動在一個月前就開始了。每個地區的
　　　周日報都有全彩夾頁廣告傳單，通常這是吸引新客戶非常
　　　有效的辦法。

主管：聽起來很有希望。

凱文：是的，我也這麼認為。尤其是我們提供最新款手機，搭配
　　　一年 32.50 美元的服務合約，簡直是沒有其他公司可以比
　　　得上。

主管：凱文，你知道我期待最高銷售額，這麼一來我們就可以再
　　　度贏得區域銷售獎。不只是我一個人獲利，所有業務代表
　　　也都有獎金可拿。

凱文：是的，我知道。相信只要再努力工作幾個月，就一定能夠
　　　再度摘冠的。

語　法

● What can I do for you?　（有什麼事嗎？）

當店員對顧客說 What can I do for you? 時，是指「歡迎光臨」的意思；
若在公司等其他地方使用 What can I do for you? 時，則是意指「有什

麼貴幹嗎?」。

- That's not bad. （還不錯。）

  not bad / not so bad / not too bad 等皆為含蓄的稱讚用法，意指「還可以」「還不錯」「並不差」。日常生活中，對於 How are you? 的問候句，也可以回答 Oh, not bad. 來表示 fine 的語意。

- Let's see. （讓我想想。）

  Let's see. 等同於 Let me see.，用於表示說話者正在思索，一時還無法馬上回答對方，是一種感嘆詞性質的用語。

Speaking Function 14

表達內心的期待

 請聽《Track 45》。

1. A: I hope to see a total sales increase of about 25%.

   B: I'd like to see that, too.

2. A: It's been raining for three days straight.

   B: I know. I hope it'll clear up soon.

3. A: I'm hoping for a quick economic recovery.

   B: So am I. Otherwise, we'll have to close one or two stores.

解說
- 對於自己內心期待、希望實現的事，英文一般是以「I hope + to 不定詞」來表達。「希望考試及格」是 I hope to pass the exam.，「期望有好結果」則是 I hope to get good results.。留意 hope 通常用於心中認定有可能實現的希望時，並不用於表達無法實現的希望。
- 要表達希望事情的發展能如自己所期待般，可以使用「I hope + (that) 子句」的構句。例如，希望生病的人「儘快康復」，就說 I hope

you get well soon.；「希望明天不會下雨」就說 I hope it won't rain tomorrow.。另外，如 I hope you (will) succeed in your work.（希望你事業成功）的 that 子句中，可以省略 will，這是當要強調希望一定能實現時而以現在式取代未來式的用法。

● I'm hoping for～ 也是表期待、希望的句型，for 之後接續對象事物。原則上，hope 不用進行式，不過若要讓語氣和緩，可使用 I'm hoping for 進行式的句型。

● 副詞 hopefully 也有表期待、希望之意，通常置於句首，意指「若是順利」「但願」「所希望的是」。

練習 1 【代換】

② 請隨《Track 46》做代換練習。

1. I hope to *get to see him while I'm in New York.*

> establish a business of my own.
> be in Los Angeles next month.
> get a job within the next three weeks.
> keep working even after I turn 60 years old.

2. I hope *we get it several days in advance.*

> everything works out for you.
> you approve of the new hallway remodeling.
> sales recover in the next few weeks.
> you succeed in your work.

3. I'm hoping for *an influx of new home buyers.*

> a three-year contract.
> the best.
> a full-time job at the company.

good results from the direct-mail campaign.

4. Hopefully, *we can solve the problem soon.*

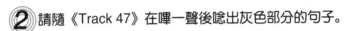
we can finish the project by December.
there will be some progress in the negotiation.
overseas sales will increase by 20% next quarter.
I'll get another one-year contract.

練習 2【角色扮演】

 請隨《Track 47》在嗶一聲後唸出灰色部分的句子。

1. A: I hope to become a lawyer when I grow up.

   B: If you keep working hard, I'm sure you will.

2. A: It's already 9 o'clock and traffic is very heavy.

   B: I hope we won't be late for the conference.

3. A: I'm hoping for an improvement in the working conditions.

   B: So am I. They are considerably below the standard right now.

練習 3【覆誦重要語句】

 請隨《Track 48》覆誦英文句子。

1. stop in 「順道經過」

   ↳Let's ask her to stop in and talk things over.

   （我們去請她過來，把事情談開。）

2. due 「到期的；應提出的」

   ↳The report is not due until the end of this month so there

is no rush. (這份報告月底才要交，所以不用急。)

3. briefing 「簡報」
   ↳An initial briefing should be presented no later than September 15 and a final report by November 30. (9 月 15 日前應作初期簡報，11 月 30 日前則須提出最後報告。)

4. off the top of one's head 「立即（不必想）就能說出的」
   ↳Well, off the top of my head, sales in March were better than sales in February.

   (嗯，我可以立即回答的是，三月份的銷售額比二月更好。)

5. according to 「根據」
   ↳According to a recent survey, most female workers in private companies are pleased with their retirement plans. (根據最近一份調查顯示，大部分私人企業的女性員工對退休金制度感到滿意。)

6. convert 「變換」
   ↳The mayor announced a plan to convert the local elementary school into a museum.

   (市長宣布一項計畫，準備將當地的小學改建為博物館。)

7. prediction 「預測，預言」
   ↳I believe the predictions of an economic recovery by the end of the year will come true.

   (我相信經濟景氣將於年底前復甦的預測會成真。)

8. probability 「機率；可能性」
   ↳The probability of the former heavyweight champion's comeback is pretty small.

   (前重量級冠軍東山再起的機會不大。)

9. kick in 「開始」

↳The sales of the new product started to increase as its TV advertising campaign kicked in. (隨著電視廣告活動的展開，新產品的銷售額也開始增加了。)

10. pull off 「獲得（獎項）」

↳A Japanese major league player pulled off the American League rookie award.

(一名日籍大聯盟選手摘下美國聯盟新人王頭銜。)

實力測驗

你是一家專門銷售進口車的汽車公司的業務員。有一天，老闆詢問你對今年的銷售業績有什麼展望。請用三種不同的說法表示自己會在一年內賣出 100 輛以上汽車的雄心壯志。

參考解答
1. I hope to sell more than 100 cars this year.
2. I hope I'll be able to sell more than 100 cars this year.
3. Hopefully, I can sell more than 100 cars this year.

| Chapter 15 | **An Epidemic Disease** | 傳染病 |

Listening

Warm-up / Pre-questions

 請聽《Track 49》的新聞報導後回答下面問題。

腦膜炎的病菌是透過什麼媒介傳染?

  (A) 空氣

  (B) 水

  (C) 唾液

內容   Two students are dead and a third is expected to recover from a shocking outbreak of meningitis in the small town of Broaden, Virginia. Janice Stanley, 15, and Ken Collins, 14, died a week ago after contracting a blood infection caused by a strain of the bacteria Neisseria meningitidis. Chris Tracy, 17, was comatose when he was admitted to Children's Valley Hospital Saturday, but is expected to recover.

The bacteria give victims meningitis, a bacterial disease that causes inflammation in the membranes that surround the brain and spinal cord. The germs are spread quickly by saliva and can be transmitted as easily as drinking out of someone's glass or eating with someone's fork. Symptoms include high fever, headaches, nausea, vomiting and exhaustion.

中譯   維吉尼亞州布羅登小鎮突然爆發腦膜炎,已有兩名學生死亡,第三名患病學生可望復原。現年 15 歲的珍妮絲・史丹利以及 14

歲的肯恩‧柯林斯，罹患由奈瑟氏腦膜炎雙球菌引發的血液感染，於一週前宣告死亡。現年 17 歲的克里斯‧崔希週六被送往溪谷兒童醫院時呈昏迷狀態，不過可望復原。

感染這種細菌讓病患罹患腦膜炎，此為細菌傳染疾病，導致大腦及脊椎附近的腦膜發炎。此種細菌擴散速度極快，傳播途徑為唾液，只要使用帶菌者用過的杯子或叉子就可能遭到感染。臨床症狀包括發燒、頭痛、噁心、嘔吐，以及全身無力。

解答 (C)

解說 英文中，數字經常用以指「人」，例如報紙標題刊登 Concorde goes down; 113 die, 即意指「協和式客機墜毀，113 個人喪生」。first, second, third 等序數詞亦可指「人」，在本新聞報導中，由於 a third 之前有出現 two students，所以 a third 是「第三個學生」之意。其他字義如下: outbreak「爆發」、meningitis「腦膜炎」、contract「染患（疾病）」、blood infection「血液感染」、cause「引起」、strain「菌種」、bacteria Neisseria meningitidis「奈瑟氏腦膜炎雙球菌」、comatose「昏迷狀態的」、admit「使入院」、victim「受害者」、bacterial「細菌的」、inflammation「炎症」、membrane「細胞膜」、spinal cord「脊髓」、saliva「唾液」、transmit「使傳染」、symptom「症狀」、fever「發燒」、nausea「噁心」、vomiting「嘔吐」，而 exhaustion 則為「筋疲力竭」之意。

Listening Step 1

 請聽《Track 50》的會話後回答下面問題。

Harris 先生和 Scott 女士正針對什麼問題討論？

　(A) 如何選擇抗生素

　(B) 如何採取預防感染腦膜炎的措施

(C) 如何治療腦膜炎患者

解答　　　　　　　　　　　　　　　　　　　　　　　　　　　(B)

Listening Step 2

熟悉下列關鍵字

regarding　關於
prompt　迅速的
obligation　義務
crisis　危機
combative　好戰的，好鬥的
approximately　大約
reside　居住
teens　十多歲（13 ～ 19 歲）的青少年
confirm　證實，確定
citizen　市民
identify　確認，識別（真相、要點）
prevention　預防
antibiotic　抗生素
clinic　門診
dose　（藥的）一劑
duty　義務
preventive　預防的
coordinate　配合
Disease Control and Prevention Department　疾病管制局
commend　讚賞
immunize　使免疫
entire　全部的；整體的

infection　感染
minimum　最小的；最低的
immunization　免疫
vaccine　疫苗
administer　實施

② 請聽《Track 51》並在括弧內填入正確答案。

1. Thank you so much for your (　　　) call.
2. Approximately how many people (　　　) in the town of Broaden?
3. Test results were (　　　) this morning, four days after the deaths.
4. I believe what is necessary here is to (　　　) the entire community.
5. We can have the (　　　) sent to you by Thursday.

解答

1. Thank you so much for your (prompt) call.

2. Approximately how many people (reside) in the town of Broaden?

3. Test results were (confirmed) this morning, four days after the deaths.

4. I believe what is necessary here is to (immunize) the entire community.

5. We can have the (vaccines) sent to you by Thursday.

② 請再聽一次《Track 50》的會話後回答下面問題。

1. 全鎮大約有多少人口?
   (A) 2,500 人
   (B) 2 萬 5 千人

(C) 25 萬人

2. 抗生素的效用可以維持多久？

  (A) 兩、三天

  (B) 一、兩個禮拜

  (C) 三年

解答	1. (B)　2. (A)

Listening Step 3

熟悉下列語句

get back with　立即與～聯絡

as you know　如你所知

What can I answer for you?　我可以提供什麼消息？你要問我什麼問題？

so far　到目前為止

over the weekend　週末期間

up to　（時間等）直到

make arrangements for　做好～準備

②請聽《Track 52》並在括弧內填入正確答案。

1. I just received your call regarding the meningitis outbreak in your town and wanted to (　　) (　　) (　　) you immediately.

2. (　　) (　　) (　　), I have an obligation to respond immediately to this crisis.

3. What action have you taken (　　) (　　) to protect the rest of the citizens?

4. The immunization will protect people for (   ) (   ) three years.

5. Can you (   ) (   ) (   ) administering the immunizations through the local high schools by then?

解答

1. I just received your call regarding the meningitis outbreak in your town and wanted to (get) (back) (with) you immediately.

2. (As) (you) (know), I have an obligation to respond immediately to this crisis.

3. What action have you taken (so) (far) to protect the rest of the citizens?

4. The immunization will protect people for (up) (to) three years.

5. Can you (make) (arrangements) (for) administering the immunizations through the local high schools by then?

②請再聽一次《Track 50》的會話後回答下面問題。

1. Scott 女士為什麼打電話給 Harris 先生？
   (A) 因為之前 Harris 先生有打電話給她
   (B) 因為須緊急通知有兩名學生死亡的消息
   (C) 因為想了解住院患者的病情

2. 對於 Harris 先生所採取的行動，Scott 女士給與什麼評價？
   (A) 有所批評
   (B) 感到不滿
   (C) 表示讚賞

3. Harris 先生今後還將採取什麼行動？
   (A) 調查感染腦膜炎的病患人數
   (B) 免費發送三萬劑抗生素

(C) 安排當地所有中學實施預防注射

| 解答 | 1. (A) 2. (C) 3. (C) |

Speaking

會話

 請再聽一次《Track 50》。

Mrs. Scott: Disease Control and Prevention Department Official
Mr. Harris: Health Department Official

＊

Mrs. Scott: Hello, Mr. Harris. I just received your call regarding the meningitis outbreak in your town and wanted to get back with you immediately.

Mr. Harris: Thank you so much for your prompt call. As you know, I have an obligation to respond immediately to this crisis.

Mrs. Scott: Yes, I understand. Let me just ask you a few questions and then we can plan our combative strategy.

Mr. Harris: Sure. What can I answer for you?

Mrs. Scott: Approximately how many people reside in the town of Broaden?

Mr. Harris: About 25,000 people.

Mrs. Scott: Does the hospitalized victim have the same strain of the bacteria as the two teens who died?

Mr. Harris: Unfortunately, yes. Test results were confirmed this morning, four days after the deaths.

Mrs. Scott: What action have you taken so far to protect the rest of the citizens?

Mr. Harris: Over the weekend we conducted a media campaign—radio, television and newspaper—identifying causes, symptoms and prevention. We also gave a free antibiotic clinic yesterday and gave out about 30,000 doses of antibiotic.

Mrs. Scott: You're of course aware that the antibiotic only provides protection for a couple of days?

Mr. Harris: Yes, but I felt it was my duty to take some type of preventive action until I could coordinate with the Disease Control and Prevention Department.

Mrs. Scott: I commend you for your quick action. I believe what is necessary here is to immunize the entire community. Three infections in such a small town as Broaden certainly meets the minimum required cases under our guidelines. The immunization will protect people for up to three years. We can have the vaccines sent to you by Thursday. Can you make arrangements for administering the immunizations through the local high schools by then?

Mr. Harris: Certainly. I'll have everything arranged by Thursday morning. Thank you for your help.

史考特女士：疾病管制局官員
哈理斯先生：衛生署官員

*

史考特：哈囉，哈理斯先生。我剛剛接到你的來電，你提到你鎮
　　　　上爆發腦膜炎，所以立即和你聯絡。

哈理斯：謝謝妳這麼快回電。妳知道的，我有責任儘快處理疫情。

史考特：是的，我了解。讓我先問你幾個問題，然後我們才能擬
　　　　定對抗疫情的策略。

哈理斯：當然，我可以提供什麼消息呢？

史考特：大約有多少人口居住在布羅登鎮？

哈理斯：約兩萬五千人。

史考特：入院患者和兩名青少年死者所感染的病菌是相同的嗎？

哈理斯：很不幸，是相同的。今天早上的檢驗結果已經證實了這
　　　　點，今天是他們死亡後的第四天。

史考特：目前為止進行了哪些措施來保護其他鎮民？

哈理斯：週末期間我們實施媒體宣傳活動，透過廣播、電視、報
　　　　紙來指導分辨病因、症狀及預防措施。昨天我們也提供
　　　　免費門診注射抗生素，共用了三萬劑抗生素。

史考特：你應當很清楚抗生素的藥效只能維持幾天。

哈理斯：是的，但我覺得和疾病管制局配合以前，我有責任先採
　　　　取一些預防措施。

史考特：你的反應迅速值得讚賞。我認為現在需要的是讓整個社
　　　　區免疫。像布羅登這麼小的鎮出現三起感染病例的情形，
　　　　確實已經達到我們指導方針中必須處理的最低標準。若

實施免疫，將可保護居民三年內不受感染。我們會在星期四之前把疫苗送過去，到時你可不可以安排當地所有中學進行疫苗接種的工作？

哈理斯：當然可以。我會在星期四早上以前把所有的事情安排好，非常感謝妳的協助。

語　法 ‥‥‥‥‥‥‥‥‥‥‥‥‥‥‥‥‥‥‥‥‥‥‥‥‥‥‥‥‥‥‥‥‥‥‥‥‥‥

● 「符合（條件等）」的 meet
  meet 除了「遇見」「相會」的意思之外，亦可作「符合（條件等）」解釋。例句如：His company's products *met* all our requirements.（他的公司產品符合我們的所有要求）。

● 關係代名詞的 what
  I believe what is necessary here is... 中出現的 what 為關係代名詞，中譯為「我認為現在需要的是…」之意。其實，在此的 what 實為包含先行詞作用的關係代名詞，文法上稱作複合關代，意指「所做～的事（物）」。

Speaking Function 15

表達義務與責任的說法

 請聽《Track 53》。

1. A: Would you like some more wine?

   B: No, thank you. I must go now.

2. A: I heard you're living with your parents.

   B: Yes. I feel it's my duty to look after them.

3. A: Would you like a cigarette?

   B: I better not. I'm cutting down on smoking.

解說

● 要將出自義務或責任的應該做的事項傳達給對方知道時，使用的基本句型是「I must + 動詞」。除了 must 外，也可以用 should, ought to, have got to, had better 等替代。have to 聽起來會比 must 的語氣柔和，多用於客觀上視為必要的場合時所說；should 的語意則比 must 弱；ought to 在表「義務」時，語意略比 should 強。上述按照義務或必要性的程度大小排列時，即為 must ＞ ought to ＞ should。另外，have got to 是 have to 的口語說法；had better 則含有「不那麼做，會造成困擾」的語感，有時亦可省略 had，說成 I better 即可。

● 我們也可以用 duty（義務，責任）這個單字來表達自己必須做的事情，例如用 It is my duty to ～，或使用語氣較為委婉客氣的 I feel it is my duty to ～來表達。另外，同義的說法為 I feel obliged to ～，其他還有 I have an obligation to ～ / I'm committed to ～ / I feel it is necessary for me to ～等等。

● 表達自己「不應該做」的說法有 I better not. / No way! / I feel it is my duty not to. / I feel obliged not to. 等。No way! 是強調說法，語意為「絕對不行」「豈有此理」。

練習 1【代換】

 請隨《Track 54》做代換練習。

1. *I must* cut down on smoking.

I have to
I should
I ought to
I've got to
I'd better

2. *I feel it is my duty to*   put him through college.

I feel obliged to

I'm obliged to

I have an obligation to

I'm committed to

I feel it is necessary for me to

3. "Would you like a cigarette?"

"*I better not. I'm cutting down on smoking.*"

"No way! My doctor told me to stop smoking completely."

"I feel it is my duty not to. My doctor told me to quit smoking."

"I feel obliged not to. I promised my wife that I would quit smoking."

練習 2【角色扮演】

 請隨《Track 55》在嗶一聲後唸出灰色部分的句子。

1. A: Would you like to see the rest of the collection?

B: No, thank you. I must go now.

2. A: I heard you're going to cooperate with us in the investigation.

B: Yes. I feel it is my duty to tell the truth.

3. A: Would you like more wine?

B: I better not. I'm cutting down on drinking.

練習 3【覆誦重要語句】

② 請隨《Track 56》覆誦英文句子。

1. regarding 「關於」
   ↳A decision must be made regarding the joint project.
   （關於這件合作計畫，必須做出一項決定。）

2. get back with 「立即與～聯絡」
   ↳I'll get back with you as soon as today's subcommittee meeting is over.
   （今天小組委員會結束後，我會儘快再和你聯絡。）

3. as you know 「如你所知」
   ↳As you know, passengers must check in 60 minutes before departure on international flights.（如你所知，搭乘國際航班的旅客必須在起飛前 60 分鐘辦理報到。）

4. approximately 「大約」
   ↳Ninety-five percent of the approximately 12 million cars scrapped each year are collected for recycling.（每年大約有一千兩百萬部的舊車報廢，其中 95% 會回收。）

5. confirm 「確認」
   ↳Would you please confirm this order in writing?
   （可否請您以書面形式確認這份訂單?）

6. identify 「確認，識別（真相、要點)」
   ↳You need to identify the problem in order to solve it.
   （你必須認清問題才能解決它。）

7. commend 「讚賞」
   ↳Mr. Scott commended his wife for her business acumen.
   （史考特先生稱讚他妻子的生意頭腦。）

8. meet 「滿足，符合（條件等）」

↳ The new network system met all their requirements.

（這個新的網路系統符合他們的所有要求。）

9. up to 「直到」

↳ People who exercise vigorously several times a week can reduce their chances of getting diabetes by up to 42 percent. （一週從事數次激烈運動的人罹患糖尿病的機率最多可以降低42%。）

10. make arrangements for 「做好～準備」

↳ Mr. Drake told his secretary to make arrangements for a dinner meeting with a group of Japanese businessmen. （德瑞克先生要他的秘書安排好與數名日籍商人的晚餐聚會。）

實力測驗

你的公司今天舉辦迎新會，熱烈歡迎新同事的加入。當聚會結束後，有同事對你說 Let's go to a karaoke bar?，邀你一同到卡拉 OK 店歡唱。你是很想去一展歌喉，但碰巧今天是女兒生日，必須早點回家。請用三種不同的說法表達不得不離開以及必須趕回家的理由。

參考解答

1. I must go home now. Today is my daughter's birthday.

2. I've got to go home now. Today is my daughter's birthday.

3. I better go home now. Today is my daughter's birthday.

An Epidemic Disease   205

動態英語文法

阿部一 著／張慧敏 譯

翻開市面上的英語文法書，可以發現大部分都是文法規則說明，繁而雜的文法概念、生硬的解說，真是令人望而生怯，難道文法只能用這種方式學習嗎？請你不妨打開本書看看，作者是以談天的方式，生動地為你解說看似枯燥無味的文法概念，扭轉文法只能死背的印象，讓人驚訝文法竟然也能這麼有趣。

活用美語修辭——老美的說話藝術

枝川公一 著／羅慧娟 譯

作者以幽默的筆調介紹美語特殊詞彙的譬喻用法，例如：belly button（肚子的鈕扣）、maggot in one's head（腦袋的蛆蟲）、mosquito cough（蚊子的咳嗽）、sell ice to Eskimos（賣冰給愛斯基摩人），這些實際意指什麼呢？作者將引用英文書報雜誌的巧言妙句為你解說，帶你徜徉於美國人的想像天地裡，享受自由聯想的語言趣味。

社交英文書信

Janusz Buda、長野格、城戶保男　著 ／ 羅慧娟　譯

欣聞友人獲獎，你會用英文書寫恭賀信函嗎？商務貿易關係若僅止於格式化的書信往返，彼此將永遠不會有深層的互動。若想進一步打好人際關係，除了訂單、出貨之外，噓寒問暖也是必須的。本書特別針對商業人士社交上的需求而編寫，內容包羅萬象，是你最佳的社交英文書信指南。

商用英文書信

高崎榮一郎、Paul Bissonnette　著

篠田義明　監修 ／ 彭士晃　譯

閑熟商業用語、精通文法句型，寫起商務英文書信來就能得心應手嗎？其實商務書信的寫作就如同作文一般，起承轉合的拿捏才是關鍵。本書從商場實務的溝通原則出發，收集商業人士的實際範例，剖析英文書信的段落架構，追求清楚的內容邏輯，更列出改善範例以供對照，是一本從事貿易工作者最佳的商用英文書信指南。

英語大考驗

小倉弘 著 / 本局編輯部 譯

想知道你的文法基礎夠紮實嗎?你以為所有的文法概念,老師在課堂上都會講到嗎?本書由日本補教界名師所執筆撰寫,將提供你一個思考英語的新觀點:學習英語文法,貴在理解,而非死背。藉由本書,重新審視之前所學的文法,將會發現:所有原本以為懂的、不懂的,或一知半解的問題,都可以在這本書裡找到答案!

打開話匣子──Small Talk一下!

L. J. Link、Nozawa Ai 著 / 何信彰 譯

雙CD

你能夠隨時用英語與人Small Talk、閒聊一番嗎?有些人在正式的商業英語溝通上儘管應對自如,但是一碰到閒話家常,卻常常手足無措。本書即針對此問題,教你從找話題到接話題的秘訣。對話臨場感十足並語帶詼諧的本書,必定讓你打開話匣子,輕鬆講英文!

國家圖書館出版品預行編目資料

英語聽&說:高級篇 / 白野伊津夫, Lisa A. Stefani著;
何信彰,鄭惠雯譯.－－初版一刷.－－臺北市;三
民，2003
　　面；　公分

ISBN 957-14-3859-6　（精裝）

1.英國語言－讀本

805.18　　　　　　　　　　　　　92009329

網路書店位址　http://www.sanmin.com.tw

ⓒ　英語聽&說
　　——高級篇

著作人　白野伊津夫　Lisa A. Stefani
譯　者　何信彰　鄭惠雯
發行人　劉振強
著作財
產權人　三民書局股份有限公司
　　　　臺北市復興北路386號
發行所　三民書局股份有限公司
　　　　地址／臺北市復興北路386號
　　　　電話／(02)25006600
　　　　郵撥／0009998-5
印刷所　三民書局股份有限公司
門市部　復北店／臺北市復興北路386號
　　　　重南店／臺北市重慶南路一段61號
初版一刷　2003年7月
編　號　S 80442-1
基本定價　陸元肆角
行政院新聞局登記證局版臺業字第○二○○號

ISBN　957-14-3859-6　（精裝）

白野伊津夫

日本明海大學副教授、明治大學講師。美國維吉尼亞大學口語傳播（Speech Communication）研究所碩士。著有多本與英語學習相關的書籍。

Lisa A. Stefani

美國加州 Grossmont College 講師。聖地牙哥州立大學碩士。亦有多本英語學習的相關著作問世。

《高級篇》CD Track 【共兩片／全部英語錄製】